[印]泰戈尔原著

飘鸟·萤火虫

Stray Birds & Fireflies

黄建滨　黄尚戎　辑译

ZHEJIANG UNIVERSITY PRESS
浙江大学出版社
·杭州·

图书在版编目(CIP)数据

飘鸟·萤火虫：汉英对照 / 黄建滨，黄尚戎辑译
. —杭州：浙江大学出版社，2022.7(2022.10 重印)
ISBN 978-7-308-22769-8

Ⅰ.①飘… Ⅱ.①黄… ②黄… Ⅲ.①汉语—英语—
对照读物 ②诗集—印度—现代 Ⅳ.①H319.4：I

中国版本图书馆 CIP 数据核字(2022)第 113144 号

飘鸟·萤火虫

黄建滨　黄尚戎　辑译

责任编辑	诸葛勤	
责任校对	黄静芬	
封面设计	周　灵	
出版发行	浙江大学出版社	
	（杭州市天目山路 148 号　邮政编码310007）	
	（网址：http://www.zjupress.com）	
排　　版	浙江时代出版服务有限公司	
印　　刷	浙江新华数码印务有限公司	
开　　本	787 mm × 1092 mm　1/32	
印　　张	12.5	
字　　数	311 千	
版 印 次	2022 年 7 月第 1 版　2022 年 10 月第 2 次印刷	
书　　号	ISBN 978-7-308-22769-8	
定　　价	68.00 元	

Contents / 目 录

飘 鸟

Stray Birds

（原著：[印]泰戈尔　黄建滨、黄尚戎译）

1

Stray birds of summer come to my window to sing and fly away. And yellow leaves of autumn, which have no songs, flutter and fall there with a sigh.

夏天的飘鸟
来到我窗前
唱着歌儿飞去。
秋天的黄叶，
没有歌可唱，
飘落到那里
一声叹息。

2

O Troupe of little vagrants of the world, leave your footprints in my words.

噢，世上这一小队
漂泊者，
请留足迹
于我文字。

3

The world puts off its mask of vastness to its lover. It becomes small as one song, as one kiss of the eternal.

世界向它爱人打开
无垠的面具。
它变得小如一首歌
小如一永恒的吻。

4

It is the tears of the earth that keep her smiles in bloom.

> 大地的眼泪
> 使她的微笑
> 美如花。

5

The mighty desert is burning for the love of a blade of grass who shakes her head and laughs and flies away.

> 浩瀚沙漠
> 为了一叶绿草的爱
> 燃烧
> 绿草摇了摇头
> 笑着
> 然后飞走。

6

If you shed tears when you miss the sun, you also miss the stars.

> 若因错过太阳哭泣，
> 你也会错过群星。

7

The sands in your way beg for your song and your movement, dancing water. Will you carry the burden of their lameness?

> 舞动的流水啊，
> 路上的泥沙
> 要你歌唱流淌。
> 你可愿携跛足的泥沙
> 前行？

8

Her wistful face haunts my dreams like the rain at night.

> 她热切的脸
> 如夜雨扰我梦乡。

9

Once we dreamt that we were strangers. We wake up to find that we were dear to each other.

> 曾梦见
> 我们不相识。
> 醒来发现
> 我们过去
> 曾彼此珍视。

10

Sorrow is hushed into peace in my heart like the evening among the silent trees.

忧思在我心中
平静下去
如暮色降临
在寂静山林。

11

Some unseen fingers, like an idle breeze, are playing upon my heart the music of the ripples.

一些看不见的手指，
如懒懒的微风，
在我心上弹奏
潺潺乐声。

12

"What language is thine, O sea?"
"The language of eternal question."
"What language is thy answer, O sky?"
"The language of eternal silence."

> "海啊，你在说什么？"
> "我说的是永恒的问题。"
> "天空啊，那你的回答呢？"
> "我说的是永恒的沉寂。"

13

Listen, my heart, to the whispers of the world with which it makes love to you.

> 听，我的心，
> 世界用她的低语
> 在向你
> 表达爱意。

14

The mystery of creation is like the darkness of night—
it is great. Delusions of knowledge are like the fog of
the morning.

创造的神秘
犹如夜间的黑暗一样——
是伟大的。
知识的幻影
却如同早晨的雾霭一样。

15

Do not seat your love upon a precipice because it is
high.

不要因峭壁高耸
便让你的爱
端坐其上。

16

I sit at my window this morning where the world like a
passer-by stops for a moment, nods to me and goes.

今晨我坐在窗前，
世界犹如一个过路的人，
停留了片刻，
点点头离去。

17

These little thoughts are the rustle of leaves; they have
their whisper of joy in my mind.

这些微思
如树叶之簌簌；
在我的心里
欢快地微语。

18

What you are you do not see, what you see is your shadow.

> 你看不见你自己，
> 看见的只是影子。

19

My wishes are fools, they shout across thy song, my Master. Let me but listen.

> 神，
> 我的愿望真蠢，
> 竟盖过你的歌声。
> 让我静静听。

20

I cannot choose the best. The best chooses me.

我不选最好的。
最好的选我。

21

They throw their shadows before them who carry their
lantern on their back.

把灯背在背上的人
他们的影子投到面前。

22

That I exist is a perpetual surprise which is life.

我的存在
是永久的奇迹
这是生命。

23

"We, the rustling leaves, have a voice that answers the storms, but who are you so silent?"

"I am a mere flower."

> "我们，婆娑树叶，
> 用声音
> 回应暴雨。
> 你是谁，
> 如此沉默？"
> "我不过是朵花。"

24

Rest belongs to the work as the eyelids to the eyes.

> 休息之于工作
> 如眼睑之于眼睛。

25

Man is a born child, his power is the power of growth.

> 人如孩子，
> 他的力量
> 是生长的力量。

26

God expects answers for the flowers he sends us, not for the sun and the earth.

> 神盼我们回应
> 他给我们以花朵，
> 而非太阳、大地。

27

The light that plays, like a naked child, among the green leaves happily knows not that man can lie.

> 光如裸体孩童，
> 在绿叶丛中欢快嬉戏，
> 浑然不知
> 人会骗人。

28

O Beauty, find thyself in love, not in the flattery of thy mirror.

> 美啊，
> 在爱中找自己，
> 不要在镜中的谄媚
> 找寻。

29

My heart beats her waves at the shore of the world and writes upon it her signature in tears with the words, "I love thee."

> 我的心泛起波浪
> 拍打着世界的海岸，
> 蘸着泪水
> 写下她的题记：
> "我爱你。"

30

"Moon, for what do you wait?"
"To salute the sun for whom I must make way."

> "月亮，
> 你在等谁？"
> "向我让位给他的太阳
> 致敬。"

31

The trees come up to my window like the yearning
voice of the dumb earth.

> 绿树长到我窗前
> 如喑哑的大地
> 喊出渴望。

32

His own mornings are new surprises to God.

> 神的清晨
> 在他看来
> 也新奇。

33

Life finds its wealth by the claims of the world, and its
worth by the claims of love.

生命因世界
找到其财富，
又因爱
找到其价值。

34

The dry river-bed finds no thanks for its past.

枯竭的河床
并不感谢过去。

35

The bird wishes it were a cloud. The cloud wishes it
were a bird.

鸟儿愿意做一片云。
云儿愿意做一只鸟。

36

The waterfall sings, "I find my song, when I find my freedom."

> 瀑布歌唱道：
> "得到自由，
> 我便放声歌唱。"

37

I cannot tell why this heart languishes in silence. It is for small needs it never asks, or knows or remembers.

> 我不明白这颗心
> 为何默默苦恼。
> 是为它不曾要求、知道、记得的
> 小需要。

38

Woman, when you move about in your household service your limbs sing like a hill stream among its pebbles.

女人，
操持家务时
你手舞足蹈
犹如山间溪水
欢唱穿过卵石。

39

The sun goes to cross the Western sea, leaving its last salutation to the East.

太阳穿过
西方的海面，
向东方表达
他最后的敬意。

40

Do not blame your food because you have no appetite.

> 不要因为没有胃口
> 而抱怨食物。

41

The trees, like the longings of the earth, stand a-tiptoe to peep at the heaven.

> 树林，
> 犹如大地的愿望，
> 踮起了脚尖
> 向天空窥望。

42

You smiled and talked to me of nothing and I felt that for this I had been waiting long.

你对我微笑
默默无语。
对我而言
却已为此等候多年。

43

The fish in the water is silent, the animal on the earth is noisy, the bird in the air is singing. But man has in him the silence of the sea, the noise of the earth and the music of the air.

水中的游鱼沉默无言，
陆地上的动物高声喧哗，
空中鸟儿欢快歌唱。
但是人类既有大海的沉默、
大地的喧闹，
也有空中的欢唱。

44

The world rushes on over the strings of the lingering
heart making the music of sadness.

> 世界
> 从踌躇满志的心弦上
> 奔跑而去
> 弹奏出
> 忧郁的音乐。

45

He has made his weapons his gods. When his weapons
win he is defeated himself.

> 他把武器
> 奉为众神。
> 武器获胜
> 他自己却败下阵来。

46

God finds himself by creating.

神从创造
发现自我。

47

Shadow, with her veil drawn, follows Light in secret meekness, with her silent steps of love.

影子，
披着面纱，
爱的脚步轻轻，
秘密且温顺
追随着光。

48

The stars are not afraid to appear like fireflies.

> 群星丝毫不怕
> 看着像萤火虫。

49

I thank thee that I am none of the wheels of power but I am one with the living creatures that are crushed by it.

> 我庆幸
> 我不是权力的
> 一个轮子
> 而是被压在权力之轮下的
> 众生之一。

50

The mind, sharp but not broad, sticks at every point but does not move.

> 心尖锐，
> 不宽广，
> 专注各点
> 却纹丝不动。

51

Your idol is shattered in the dust to prove that God's dust is greater than your idol.

> 你的偶像
> 碎为尘埃
> 证明神的尘埃
> 比你的偶像伟大。

52

Man does not reveal himself in his history, he struggles up through it.

> 人无法在历史中
> 表现他自己，
> 只能奋斗前行。

53

While the glass lamp rebukes the earthen for calling it cousin, the moon rises, and the glass lamp, with a bland smile, calls her, "My dear, dear sister."

> 玻璃灯责备陶土灯叫它表妹。
> 明月升起，
> 玻璃灯却微笑着呼唤：
> "亲爱的，亲爱的姐姐。"

54

Like the meeting of the seagulls and the waves we meet and come near. The seagulls fly off, the waves roll away and we depart.

> 如海鸥与浪花相遇
> 我们相遇，走在一起。
> 海鸥飞去，
> 浪花散去
> 我们也分离。

55

My day is done, and I am like a boat drawn on the beach, listening to the dance-music of the tide in the evening.

> 白昼退去，
> 我像一只海滩上的小船，
> 聆听着傍晚潮水
> 拍打出的舞曲之声。

56

Life is given to us, we earn it by giving it.

> 我们的命
> 天赐，
> 唯献出
> 方能获取。

57

We come nearest to the great when we are great in humility.

> 我们大为谦卑时
> 便是最近伟大之际。

58

The sparrow is sorry for the peacock at the burden of
its tail.

麻雀看见孔雀
沉重的翎尾
为它担心不已。

59

Never be afraid of the moments—thus sings the voice
of the everlasting.

绝不要害怕
那些瞬间——
永恒的声音
在这样歌唱。

60

The hurricane seeks the shortest road by the no-road,
and suddenly ends its search in the Nowhere.

> 于无路之中
> 飓风寻求最短之途，
> 在"乌有之地"
> 突然停止追求。

61

Take my wine in my own cup, friend. It loses its
wreath of foam when poured into that of others.

> 在我杯中饮酒，
> 朋友。
> 一倒进他人酒杯
> 这酒的飞沫便消失。

62

The Perfect decks itself in beauty for the love of the Imperfect.

> 完美把自己打扮美丽
> 向不完美表示爱意。

63

God says to man, "I heal you therefore I hurt, love you therefore punish."

> 神对人说：
> "我救你所以伤你，
> 爱你所以罚你。"

64

Thank the flame for its light, but do not forget the lampholder standing in the shade with constancy of patience.

感谢火焰给你光明，
但不要忘了灯座
是它
耐心坚毅
挺立于黑暗中。

65

Tiny grass, your steps are small, but you possess the
earth under your tread.

小草呀，
你的步履虽小，
却拥有足下的大地。

66

The infant flower opens its bud and cries, "Dear World,
please do not fade."

幼花蓓蕾绽放，喊道：
"亲爱的世界，
请别凋谢。"

67

God grows weary of great kingdoms, but never of little
flowers.

神厌恶伟大的帝国，
但绝不厌恶小花朵。

68

Wrong cannot afford defeat but Right can.

错误难抵失败，
真理无敌。

69

"I give my whole water in joy," sings the waterfall,
"though little of it is enough for the thirsty."

瀑布歌唱道：
"我快乐地给你全部的水，
虽然为解渴你只需少许。"

70

Where is the fountain that throws up these flowers in a
ceaseless outbreak of ecstasy?

把花抛起
让它们不断绽放狂喜的源泉
到底在哪里？

71

The woodcutter's axe begged for its handle from the tree. The tree gave it.

> 樵夫的斧头
> 向树祈求斧头手柄。
> 树随其愿。

72

In my solitude of heart I feel the sigh of this widowed evening veiled with mist and rain.

> 在我孤寂的心里
> 我感觉到
> 雨雾绵绵
> 寡独黄昏的叹息。

73

Chastity is a wealth that comes from abundance of love.

> 贞操
> 是丰裕的爱情
> 生出来的财富。

74

The mist, like love, plays upon the heart of the hills and brings out surprises of beauty.

> 雾像爱情,
> 在山峦的心上嬉戏
> 生出种种美丽的惊喜。

75

We read the world wrong and say that it deceives us.

我们误读世界
却说它是骗子。

76

The poet wind is out over the sea and the forest to seek his own voice.

诗人之风
飘过大海和森林
去追寻
自己的声音。

77

Every child comes with the message that God is not yet discouraged of man.

每个孩子出生
都会带信
神对人类
还未死心。

78

The grass seeks her crowd in the earth. The tree seeks his solitude of the sky.

> 小草追求地上的热闹。
> 大树追求天空的孤傲。

79

Man barricades against himself.

> 人对自己
> 筑起堤防。

80

Your voice, my friend, wanders in my heart, like the muffled sound of the sea among these listening pines.

> 朋友，你的声音，

萦绕我心，
像大海低吟
回荡在静听的松林中。

81

What is this unseen flame of darkness whose sparks
are the stars?

火花是繁星
无形暗火
到底是什么？

82

Let life be beautiful like summer flowers and death like
autumn leaves.

让生命
如夏花般灿烂
让死
如秋叶般安详。

83

He who wants to do good knocks at the gate; he who loves finds the gate open.

> 想做好人的人在外敲门；
> 爱的人发现门开了。

84

In death the many becomes one; in life the one becomes many. Religion will be one when God is dead.

> 死时
> 众多合而为一；
> 生时
> 一变化为众多。
> 神死了
> 宗教便合而为一。

85

The artist is the lover of Nature, therefore he is her
slave and her master.

> 艺术家是大自然的情人，
> 就是她的奴隶
> 她的主人。

86

"How far are you from me, O Fruit?"
"I am hidden in your heart, O Flower."

> "你离我多远，果儿啊？"
> "我藏在你的心里，花儿呀。"

87

This longing is for the one who is felt in the dark, but
not seen in the day.

这渴望
是为在黑夜能感到，
但白天看不到的人。

88

"You are the big drop of dew under the lotus leaf, I am
the smaller one on its upper side," said the dewdrop to
the lake.

露珠对湖水说道：
　"你是荷叶下面那颗
大大的露珠，
我是荷叶上面
小小的露珠。"

89

The scabbard is content to be dull when it protects the
keenness of the sword.

刀鞘满足于自己的迟钝
但保护了刀刃的锋利。

90

In darkness the One appears as uniform; in the light the
One appears as manifold.

> 在黑暗中
> "一"显露出单一化；
> 在光明中
> "一"显露出多元化。

91

The great earth makes herself hospitable with the help
of the grass.

> 大地以其芳草茵茵
> 尽显殷勤好客之道。

92

The birth and death of the leaves are the rapid whirls of the eddy whose wider circles move slowly among stars.

> 绿叶的生死
> 是旋风的急转
> 它更宽广的旋转
> 是在群星间缓缓移动。

93

Power said to the world, "You are mine."
The world kept it prisoner on her throne.
Love said to the world, "I am thine."
The world gave it the freedom of her house.

> 权力怼世界："你是我的。"
> 世界把它关在她宝座下。
> 爱情说道："我是你的。"
> 世界给予爱情家的自由。

94

The mist is like the earth's desire. It hides the sun for
whom she cries.

浓雾仿佛大地所望，
藏起它渴求的太阳。

95

Be still, my heart, these great trees are prayers.

心啊，安静，
大树正在祈祷。

96

The noise of the moment scoffs at the music of the Eternal.

此刻的喧嚣正在嘲笑
永恒的神的音乐。

97

I think of other ages that floated upon the stream of life and love and death and are forgotten, and I feel the freedom of passing away.

> 想起漂浮在生死
> 与爱的溪流上的
> 其他时代
> 它们已经被遗忘，
> 我感到了离开尘世的
> 自由。

98

The sadness of my soul is her bride's veil. It waits to be lifted in the night.

> 我心悲伤
> 是她新娘面纱。
> 面纱在等待夜
> 揭开它。

99

Death's stamp gives value to the coin of life; making it
possible to buy with life what is truly precious.

死的印章
给生命之币价值；
使它能用生命去购买
确有价值之物。

100

The cloud stood humbly in a corner of the sky. The
morning crowned it with splendour.

白云谦逊地站在
天空的一角。
黎明为它
披上彩霞。

101

The dust receives insult and in return offers her flowers.

尘土受到侮辱
却以其花朵作为回报。

102

Do not linger to gather flowers to keep them, but walk on, for flowers will keep themselves blooming all your way.

不要为了采集鲜花
停留下来，
向前走，
一路上都会有鲜花
不断绽放。

103

Roots are the branches down in the earth. Branches are roots in the air.

> 树根是地下的树枝。
> 树枝是空中的树根。

104

The music of the far-away summer flutters around the autumn seeking its former nest.

> 远去了的夏日的音乐
> 在秋天里翱翔
> 寻找它过去的
> 巢穴。

105

Do not insult your friend by lending him merits from your own pocket.

别把自己袋里的功绩
借给朋友
这是污辱。

106

The touch of the nameless days clings to my heart like mosses round the old tree.

无名岁月的感触
附于我心
如苔藓环绕老树。

107

The echo mocks her origin to prove she is the original.

回声嘲笑她的原声
以此证明她是原声。

108

God is ashamed when the prosperous boasts of His special favour.

当成功者炫耀神的特惠时
神深感羞愧。

109

I cast my own shadow upon my path, because I have a lamp that has not been lighted.

我把我的影子
投射在路上，
只因我有一盏灯
还没点亮。

110

Man goes into the noisy crowd to drown his own clamour of silence.

> 人走进喧闹的人群
> 要淹没他沉默的呐喊。

111

That which ends in exhaustion is death, but the perfect ending is in the endless.

> 终止于衰竭的
> 是死亡,
> 圆满的结局在于
> 永无止境。

112

The sun has his simple robe of light. The clouds are decked with gorgeousness.

太阳穿着朴素的光衣。
白云衣装绚丽无比。

113

The hills are like shouts of children who raise their arms, trying to catch stars.

> 山峰
> 如孩童喧闹
> 举起双臂，
> 想去捉星星。

114

The road is lonely in its crowd for it is not loved.

> 道路拥挤但寂寞
> 因为没得到爱。

115

The power that boasts of its mischiefs is laughed at by the yellow leaves that fall, and clouds that pass by.

> 权力夸耀其恶行
> 却遭到飘落的黄叶
> 与飘过的白云的
> 嘲笑。

116

The earth hums to me today in the sun, like a woman at her spinning, some ballad of the ancient time in a forgotten tongue.

> 今天大地在阳光下
> 向我吟唱，
> 如织布的妇人，
> 用一种被忘却的语言
> 哼着古代歌谣。

117

The grass-blade is worthy of the great world where it grows.

> 草叶
> 无愧它所生长的
> 伟大世界。

118

Dream is a wife who must talk. Sleep is a husband who silently suffers.

> 梦是饶舌的妻子。
> 睡眠是默默忍受的丈夫。

119

The night kisses the fading day whispering to his ear, "I am death, your mother. I am to give you fresh birth."

黑夜亲吻将逝的白天
对它低语：
"我是死神，你母亲。
我要给你新生命。"

120

I feel thy beauty, dark night, like that of the loved
woman when she has put out the lamp.

黑夜，
我感觉到你的美，
犹如熄灯后
可爱的妇人。

121

I carry in my world that flourishes the worlds that have
failed.

我把已逝世界的繁荣
带进我的世界。

122

Dear friend, I feel the silence of your great thoughts of
many a deepening eventide on this beach when I listen
to these waves.

> 亲爱的朋友，
> 静听涛声
> 我感受到海岸上
> 无数暮色黄昏中
> 你伟大思想的沉默。

123

The bird thinks it is an act of kindness to give the fish a
life in the air.

> 鸟儿以为
> 在空中给鱼儿生命
> 是一种慈善之举。

124

"In the moon thou sendest thy love letters to me," said the night to the sun. "I leave my answers in tears upon the grass."

夜对太阳说道:
"你在月下把情书给我,
我在绿草上
含泪给你留下了答复。"

125

The Great is a born child; when he dies he gives his great childhood to the world.

伟人生为赤子,
死时他把伟大童年
留给世界。

126

Not hammer-strokes, but dance of the water sings the
pebbles into perfection.

不是锤击，
而是水的歌舞
使得鹅卵石
趋于完美。

127

Bees sip honey from flowers and hum their thanks
when they leave. The gaudy butterfly is sure that the
flowers owe thanks to him.

蜜蜂从花中啜蜜
离开时嘤嘤道谢。
浮华的蝴蝶却认定
花儿应该向他道谢。

128

To be outspoken is easy when you do not wait to speak the complete truth.

如果你等不及说出全部事实
直言不讳很容易。

129

Asks the Possible to the Impossible, "Where is your dwelling-place?"
"In the dreams of the impotent," comes the answer.

"可能"有一次
向"不可能"发问：
"你住什么地方？"
答案是：
"在无能为力者的梦里。"

130

If you shut your door to all errors truth will be shut out.

> 若把错误都挡门外
> 真理也将被挡。

131

I hear some rustle of things behind my sadness of heart,
—I cannot see them.

> 我听见
> 我悲伤的心情后有沙沙声，
> ——但我看不到。

132

Leisure in its activity is work.
The stillness of the sea stirs in waves.

闲暇在活动时便是工作。
海水静止动荡成波涛。

133

The leaf becomes flower when it loves. The flower
becomes fruit when it worships.

绿叶恋爱时便开成花。
花儿崇拜时便结成果实。

134

The roots below the earth claim no rewards for making
the branches fruitful.

地底下的树根
使大树硕果累累
却不求回报。

135

This rainy evening the wind is restless. I look at the swaying branches and ponder over the greatness of all things.

> 阴雨的黄昏，
> 风无休无止。
> 看着摇曳的树枝，
> 我深深感叹
> 世间万物的伟大。

136

Storm of midnight, like a giant child awakened in the untimely dark, has begun to play and shout.

> 子夜风雨，
> 如在不合时宜的暗夜
> 惊醒的巨童，
> 开始嬉戏喧闹。

137

Thou raisest thy waves vainly to follow thy lover, O
sea, thou lonely bride of the storm.

> 海啊，
> 暴风雨孤独的新娘，
> 你掀起波浪追随情郎
> 却枉然。

138

"I am ashamed of my emptiness," said the Word to the Work.
"I know how poor I am when I see you," said the Work to
the Word.

> 文字对作品说：
> "我为我的空虚而惭愧。"
> 作品对文字说：
> "看见你，
> 我便知道我多贫乏。"

139

Time is the wealth of change, but the clock in its parody makes it mere change and no wealth.

> 时间是变化的财富，
> 时钟滑稽模仿，
> 只有变化无财富。

140

Truth in her dress finds facts too tight. In fiction she moves with ease.

> 真理穿衣
> 受到约束。
> 若虚构
> 活动轻松。

141

When I travelled to here and to there, I was tired of thee. O Road, but now when thou leadest me to everywhere I am wedded to thee in love.

> 曾经我到处旅行之时，
> 我真厌倦了你。
> 路啊，
> 如今你带着我
> 去往各地
> 我爱上了你
> 嫁给了你。

142

Let me think that there is one among those stars that guides my life through the dark unknown.

> 我想
> 群星中定有一颗
> 引我走出
> 人生未知的黑暗。

143

Woman, with the grace of your fingers you touched my
things and order came out like music.

女人，
你美丽的手指
触碰我的所有，
秩序如音乐流畅。

144

One sad voice has its nest among the ruins of the years.
It sings to me in the night, —"I loved you."

一个忧郁的声音
筑巢于岁月废墟。
在夜里向我唱：
——"我爱过你。"

145

The flaming fire warns me off by its own glow. Save
me from the dying embers hidden under ashes.

> 明火以烈焰警告我
> 别靠近。
> 把我从灰烬下的余火中
> 拯救出来。

146

I have my stars in the sky, but oh for my little lamp
unlit in my house.

> 我拥有群星满天，
> 但我房间里的小灯
> 却未点燃。

147

The dust of the dead words clings to thee. Wash thy soul with silence.

逝去文字的尘埃缠你。
沉默洗净灵魂。

148

Gaps are left in life through which comes the sad music of death.

生命缝隙里传来
死亡的忧郁音乐。

149

The world has opened its heart of light in the morning. Come out, my heart, with thy love to meet it.

早晨
世界敞开了它的光明之心。
来，我的心，
带着爱去相会。

150

My thoughts shimmer with these shimmering leaves and my heart sings with the touch of this sunlight; my life is glad to be floating with all things into the blue of space, into the dark of time.

我的思绪随闪耀绿叶
闪耀；
我的心因阳光触动
歌唱；
我的生命
与万物同游蓝天
进入黑暗时间，
变得无比欢畅。

151

God's great power is in the gentle breeze, not in the storm.

> 神之威
> 是在和风中，
> 而不在暴雨里。

152

This is a dream in which things are all loose and they oppress. I shall find them gathered in thee when I awake and shall be free.

> 梦中万物散漫松懈
> 令我倍感压抑。
> 醒来发现一切聚集于你
> 感到自由无比。

153

"Who is there to take up my duties?" asked the setting sun.
"I shall do what I can, my Master," said the earthen
lamp.

落日问道：
"有谁能够继承我的使命？"
陶土灯答道：
"我一定尽我所能，主人。"

154

By plucking her petals you do not gather the beauty of
the flower.

你可以摘下花瓣
但是很难采摘到花的美丽。

155

Silence will carry your voice like the nest that holds the
sleeping birds.

> 沉默载蕴你的声音
> 正如鸟巢怀抱睡鸟。

156

The Great walks with the Small without fear.
The Middling keeps aloof.

> 伟大不怕与渺小同行。
> 庸者避而远之。

157

The night opens the flowers in secret and allows the
day to get thanks.

黑夜悄悄让花儿绽放
却让白昼去接受感恩。

158

Power takes as ingratitude the writhings of its victims.

权势认为
受害者的痛苦
是忘恩负义。

159

When we rejoice in our fulness, then we can part with our fruits with joy.

当我们以充实为乐，
便能快乐地舍弃果实。

160

The raindrops kissed the earth and whispered, —"We are thy homesick children, mother, come back to thee from the heaven."

> 雨点亲吻大地，低语：
> ——"母亲，
> 我们是你思家之子，
> 从天上回到你这里。"

161

The cobweb pretends to catch dewdrops and catches flies.

> 蛛网假装捉露珠
> 却捉住了苍蝇。

162

Love! When you come with the burning lamp of pain in your hand, I can see your face and know you as bliss.

爱情！
你手执燃亮的痛苦之灯走来，
看见你的脸
我知你幸福。

163

"The learned say that your lights will one day be no more," said the firefly to the stars. The stars made no answer.

萤火虫对群星道：
"学者说
你们的光
总有一天会熄。"
星星不予回答。

164

In the dusk of the evening the bird of some early dawn
comes to the nest of my silence.

> 在黄昏的微光里
> 一些清晨的鸟儿
> 飞到我寂静的巢穴。

165

Thoughts pass in my mind like flocks of ducks in the
sky. I hear the voice of their wings.

> 思想掠过我心
> 如群雁掠苍穹。
> 我听见
> 振翼之声。

166

The canal loves to think that rivers exist solely to supply it with water.

运河总喜欢想
江河的存在
只是为向它供给水流。

167

The world has kissed my soul with its pain, asking for its return in songs.

世界以痛苦吻我灵魂，
而要我以歌声回报。

168

That which oppresses me, is it my soul trying to come out in the open, or the soul of the world knocking at my heart for its entrance?

压迫着我的，
到底是我想要外出的灵魂，
还是敲着我的心门想要进来的
世界的灵魂？

169

Thought feeds itself with its own words and grows.

思想以己之言
养大自己。

170

I have dipped the vessel of my heart into this silent hour; it has filled with love.

当我把心的血管
浸入这宁静的时刻；
它充满了爱。

171

Either you have work or you have not. When you have
to say, "Let us do something," then begins mischief.

> 不管你是不是在工作，
> 当你无奈道，
> "我们做事吧"，
> 胡闹便开始。

172

The sunflower blushed to own the nameless flower as
her kin. The sun rose and smiled on it, saying, "Are
you well, my darling?"

> 向日葵羞于
> 把无名的花朵
> 看作同胞。
> 太阳升起
> 向它微笑道：
> "你好吗，宝贝儿？"

173

"Who drives me forward like fate?"
"The Myself striding on my back."

　"谁如命运催我行？"
　"自我在身后大步走。"

174

The clouds fill the water-cups of the river, hiding themselves in the distant hills.

　云儿把水斟满
　江河的水杯，
　自己却躲进
　远山之中。

175

I spill water from my water-jar as I walk on my way.
Very little remains for my home.

> 一路走来
> 水罐中的水
> 不断泼洒出来。
>
> 回到家
> 只剩下一点点。

176

The water in a vessel is sparkling; the water in the sea
is dark. The small truth has words that are clear; the
great truth has great silence.

> 杯中的水发出闪闪光辉；
> 海中的水泛着黑色。
> 小理文字可以说清；
> 大理却只有缄默。

177

Your smile was the flowers of your own fields, your talk was the rustle of your own mountain pines, but your heart was the woman that we all know.

你的微笑是你田园的花，
你的言谈是你山上松林沙沙，
你的心是我们认识的女子。

178

It is the little things that I leave behind for my loved ones, great things are for everyone.

这些小小的礼物
留给我所爱的人，
大的礼物留给众人。

179

Woman, thou hast encircled the world's heart with the

depth of thy tears as the sea has the earth.

> 女人，你用泪海
> 环抱着世界之心
> 正如大海
> 环绕着大地。

180

The sunshine greets me with a smile. The rain, his sad
sister, talks to my heart.

> 太阳微笑向我问候。
> 雨，他忧郁之妹，
> 和我谈心。

181

My flower of the day dropped its petals forgotten. In
the evening it ripens into a golden fruit of memory.

白昼之花
落下它被遗忘的花瓣。
黄昏中，
这花儿成熟为一颗
记忆的金色果实。

182

I am like the road in the night listening to the footfalls
of its memories in silence.

就像那晚间的道路
我在静悄悄地谛听着
记忆的脚步。

183

The evening sky to me is like a window, and a lighted
lamp, and a waiting behind it.

黄昏的天空于我，
像一扇窗，
像一盏明灯，
和那灯后的等待。

184

He who is too busy doing good finds no time to be
good.

急于做好事的人
找不到时间做好人。

185

I am the autumn cloud, empty of rain, see my fulness
in the field of ripened rice.

我是秋云，
空无雨水，
在成熟的稻田里
看见我的充实。

186

They hated and killed and men praised them. But God in shame hastens to hide its memory under the green grass.

> 他们嫉妒杀戮
> 获得赞颂。
> 神为此蒙羞
> 匆匆将其记忆埋在绿草中。

187

Toes are the fingers that have forsaken their past.

> 脚趾
> 是舍弃了其过去的
> 手指。

188

Darkness travels towards light, but blindness towards death.

> 黑暗向光明旅行，
> 盲目走向死亡。

189

The pet dog suspects the universe for scheming to take its place.

> 宠物狗怀疑宇宙耍阴谋
> 要夺它的地位。

190

Sit still, my heart, do not raise your dust. Let the world find its way to you.

静坐着，
我的心，
别扬尘。
让世界自己走向你。

191

The bow whispers to the arrow before it speeds forth—
"Your freedom is mine."

弓在箭就要射出前
对它低语——
"你的自由归我。"

192

Woman, in your laughter you have the music of the
fountain of life.

女人，
你的笑声里充溢着
生命之泉的音乐。

193

A mind all logic is like a knife all blade. It makes the
hand bleed that uses it.

> 头脑充满了逻辑，
> 犹如利刃，
> 让使用者手上流血。

194

God loves man's lamp-lights better than his own great
stars.

> 神爱人间灯火
> 甚于他的巨星。

195

This world is the world of wild storms kept tame with
the music of beauty.

这世界
是为音乐美驯服的
暴风雨的世界。

196

"My heart is like the golden casket of thy kiss," said
the sunset cloud to the sun.

晚霞对太阳说道：
"我的心
犹如你吻过的
金色宝盒。"

197

By touching you may kill, by keeping away you may
possess.

亲近
你会杀戮；

远离
你或许会去占有。

198

The cricket's chirp and the patter of rain come to me through the dark, like the rustle of dreams from my past youth.

蟋蟀唧唧
夜雨滴答
从黑暗中传来，
好似我已逝青春的
梦的窸窣。

199

"I have lost my dewdrop," cries the flower to the morning sky that has lost all its stars.

花朵哭诉，
向着星辰落尽的清晨天空：
"我丢失了露珠。"

200

The burning log bursts in flame and cries, —"This is my flower, my death."

> 火光中
> 木块大叫：
> ——"我的死神，
> 这是我的花。"

201

The wasp thinks that the honey-hive of the neighbouring bees is too small. His neighbours ask him to build one still smaller.

> 在黄蜂看来
> 邻居蜜蜂家的蜂巢
> 实在太小。
> 蜜蜂要他去
> 建一个更小的。

202

"I cannot keep your waves," says the bank to the river.
"Let me keep your footprints in my heart."

> 岸对河说：
> "你的波浪我留不住。
> 让我把你足迹
> 留在心底。"

203

The day, with the noise of this little earth, drowns the
silence of all worlds.

> 白昼，
> 以小小地球的喧扰，
> 淹没世界的沉默。

204

The song feels the infinite in the air, the picture in the earth, the poem in the air and the earth;

For its words have meaning that walks and music that soars.

歌在空中感到无限，
画在地上感到无限，
诗在两处都能感受；
诗句
有奔走的意义
飞翔的乐曲。

205

When the sun goes down to the West, the East of his morning stands before him in silence.

太阳在西方落下时，
他早晨的东方
已静静站在面前。

206

Let me not put myself wrongly to my world and set it against me.

别让我错置于自我世界
而使它与我为敌。

207

Praise shames me, for I secretly beg for it.

荣誉羞辱我，
我却暗中渴求。

208

Let my doing nothing when I have nothing to do become untroubled in its depth of peace like the evening in the seashore when the water is silent.

当我无事可做时
就让我在宁静深处
不受打扰
任何事情都不做
犹如海水沉默时
海边的暮色。

209

Maiden, your simplicity, like the blueness of the lake,
reveals your depth of truth.

少女啊，
你的单纯，
如湖水碧蓝，
凸显你真实的深度。

210

The best does not come alone. It comes with the
company of the all.

最佳之事不会独往。
它与万事万物结伴来。

211

God's right hand is gentle, but terrible is his left hand.

神的右手温柔，
他的左手却很可怕。

212

My evening came among the alien trees and spoke in a language which my morning stars did not know.

我的夜晚
来自远方
陌生树林
说的语言
我的晨星
无法听懂。

213

Night's darkness is a bag that bursts with the gold of the dawn.

> 夜之黑暗
> 如口袋
> 迸出黎明的金光。

214

Our desire lends the colours of the rainbow to the mere mists and vapours of life.

> 我们的欲望
> 把彩虹的炫彩
> 借给充满雾霭蒸汽的人生。

215

God waits to win back his own flowers as gifts from
man's hands.

> 神等着
> 从人类手中
> 赢回礼物之花。

216

My sad thoughts tease me asking me their own names.

> 忧思逗弄我
> 问自己的名字。

217

The service of the fruit is precious, the service of the
flower is sweet, but let my service be the service of the
leaves in its shade of humble devotion.

果实的奉献珍贵无比，
花儿的奉献美妙甜蜜，
让我做出绿叶的奉献吧
我要谦逊地奉上
自己的绿荫。

218

My heart has spread its sails to the idle winds for the shadowy island of Anywhere.

乘着懒散的风
我的心扬帆
驶向无处不在的
虚幻之岛。

219

Men are cruel, but Man is kind.

群氓残暴，
人类善良。

220

Make me thy cup and let my fulness be for thee and for thine.

把我当你的杯
为你和你的人斟满杯。

221

The storm is like the cry of some god in pain whose love the earth refuses.

暴风雨
像个天神在痛哭
他的爱
被大地拒绝。

222

The world does not leak because death is not a crack.

世界不会流失
死亡不是缝隙。

223

Life has become richer by the love that has been lost.

因为有爱的付出
生命更加富足。

224

My friend, your great heart shone with the sunrise of
the East like the snowy summit of a lonely hill in the
dawn.

朋友，你伟大的心
和东方旭日一起闪耀
如黎明中
孤山积雪的峰顶。

225

The fountain of death makes the still water of life play.

死亡的源泉
使生命的死水流淌。

226

Those who have everything but thee, my God, laugh at
those who have nothing but thyself.

神啊，拥有一切而没有您的人，
讥笑除您无它的人。

227

The movement of life has its rest in its own music.

生命的运动
在自己音乐里歇息。

228

Kicks only raise dust and not crops from the earth.

踢踏只扬起尘土
没有收获。

229

Our names are the light that glows on the sea waves at
night and then dies without leaving its signature.

我们的名字
是那深夜海浪上
闪烁的微光
痕迹不留
转瞬即逝。

230

Let him only see the thorns who has eyes to see the rose.

> 让看玫瑰花的人
> 也看看玫瑰的刺。

231

Set the bird's wings with gold and it will never again soar in the sky.

> 鸟翼系上黄金
> 它便永不能
> 再在天上翱翔。

232

The same lotus of our clime blooms here in the alien water with the same sweetness, under another name.

故乡的荷花
在这陌生的水域绽放
发出同样的清香，
只是换了名字。

233

In heart's perspective the distance looms large.

自心的角度
距离更遥远。

234

The moon has her light all over the sky, her dark spots to herself.

月亮把光明照遍夜空，
只留黑斑给自己。

235

Do not say, "It is morning," and dismiss it with a name of yesterday. See it for the first time as a newborn child that has no name.

> 不要说
> "这是早晨",
> 然后以昨日之名
> 把它抛弃。
> 初次相见
> 把它当作
> 没名字的新生儿。

236

Smoke boasts to the sky, and ashes to the earth, that they are brothers to the fire.

> 烟对天夸口,
> 灰对地夸口,

都视自己为
火的兄弟。

237

The raindrop whispered to the jasmine, "Keep me in
your heart for ever." The jasmine sighed, "Alas," and
dropped to the ground.

> 雨点对着茉莉花微语：
> "让我永远在你心里。"
> "唉，"茉莉花叹道，
> 落到了地上。

238

Timid thoughts, do not be afraid of me. I am a poet.

> 腆怯的思想，
> 不要怕我。
> 我是个诗人。

239

The dim silence of my mind seems filled with crickets' chirp—the grey twilight of sound.

我心中的幽静
似满是蟋蟀唧唧——
声音灰暗微明。

240

Rockets, your insult to the stars follows yourself back to the earth.

烟花，
你对群星的侮辱
又随你回到大地。

241

Thou hast led me through my crowded travels of the day to my evening's loneliness. I wait for its meaning through the stillness of the night.

> 您曾领我穿过
> 白天拥挤的旅程
> 来到黄昏的孤独。
> 我等待它的意义
> 穿过夜的寂静。

242

This life is the crossing of a sea, where we meet in the same narrow ship. In death we reach the shore and go to our different worlds.

> 这一生如漂洋过海，
> 我们相聚在同一条窄舟。
> 死时我们到达彼岸
> 去往各自世界。

243

The stream of truth flows through its channels of mistakes.

真理小溪
流过无数错误之壑。

244

My heart is homesick today for the one sweet hour
across the sea of time.

今日
我心思乡
只为跨时间之海的
甜蜜时刻。

245

The bird-song is the echo of the morning light back
from the earth.

鸟的啼鸣
是晨曦重新回到大地的
回音。

246

"Are you too proud to kiss me?" the morning light asks
the buttercup.

　　"你如此骄傲
　　不肯和我接吻？"
　　晨光问毛茛。

247

"How may I sing to thee and worship, O Sun!" asked
the little flower. "By the simple silence of thy purity,"
answered the sun.

　　"啊！太阳，
　　我该怎样歌颂你
　　崇拜你？"
　　小花问道。
　　"就用你纯洁而简朴的
　　沉静。"
　　太阳回答。

248

Man is worse than an animal when he is an animal.

当人成为禽兽之时
他比禽兽还不如。

249

Dark clouds become heaven's flowers when kissed by light.

被阳光亲吻
乌云变成天之花。

250

Let not the sword-blade mock its handle for being blunt.

千万别让剑刃嘲笑
剑柄的厚钝。

251

The night's silence, like a deep lamp, is burning with
the light of its milky way.

夜的沉默，
如深色的灯盏，
随着银河的光
而燃亮。

252

Around the sunny island of life swells day and night
death's limitless song of the sea.

大海无限的
死亡之歌
在生命光明岛四周
日夜环绕。

253

Is not this mountain like a flower, with its petals of hills,
drinking the sunlight?

> 这山
> 不是像花一样吗？
> 用峰顶的花瓣，
> 啜饮着阳光。

254

The real with its meaning read wrong and emphasis
misplaced is the unreal.

> 真实的意义被误读
> 轻重错置
> 就成了不真实。

255

Find your beauty, my heart, from the world's movement, like the boat that has the grace of the wind and
the water.

> 我的心，
> 从世界的流动，
> 找你的美，
> 正如小船得到
> 风与水的恩赐。

256

The eyes are not proud of their sight but of their
eyeglasses.

> 眼不以视力为傲
> 却以其眼镜为傲。

257

I live in this little world of mine and am afraid to make it the least less. Lift me into thy world and let me have the freedom gladly to lose my all.

我住在这小小的世界
生怕使它
再缩小一点点。
把我举到你的世界
让我自由
乐于失去我所有。

258

The false can never grow into truth by growing in power.

在权力中生长的虚假
无法变成真理。

259

My heart, with its lapping waves of song, longs to caress this green world of the sunny day.

> 我的心，
> 随歌的拍岸之浪，
> 渴望抚爱
> 暖日的绿色世界。

260

Wayside grass, love the star, then your dreams will come out in flowers.

> 路边草，
> 爱星星，
> 你的梦
> 便在花中实现。

261

Let your music, like a sword, pierce the noise of the market to its heart.

让你的音乐，
如利剑，
刺入市井
喧闹的心脏。

262

The trembling leaves of this tree touch my heart like the fingers of an infant child.

这棵树的颤动之叶
如婴儿手指
触动着我的心。

263

The little flower lies in the dust. It sought the path of
the butterfly.

> 美丽的小花
> 躺在土中，
> 它找到了
> 蝴蝶的行踪。

264

I am in the world of the roads. The night comes. Open
thy gate, thou world of the home.

> 我在道路纵横的世界。
> 夜来了。
> 开门吧，
> 如家的世界。

265

I have sung the songs of thy day. In the evening let me
carry thy lamp through the stormy path.

> 我唱了您白天的歌。
> 夜晚让我提着您的灯
> 穿过风雨之路。

266

I do not ask thee into the house.
Come into my infinite loneliness, my Lover.

> 我不求你走进我的屋。
> 亲爱的，
> 请你走进我
> 无尽的孤独。

267

Death belongs to life as birth does. The walk is in the raising of the foot as in the laying of it down.

与生一样
死属于生。
把脚抬起是走路
正如把脚落下
也还是走路。

268

I have learnt the simple meaning of thy whispers in flowers and sunshine—teach me to know thy words in pain and death.

我已懂得花与阳光里
低语的简明含义——
再教我明白
你话中的苦与死。

269

The night's flower was late when the morning kissed her, she shivered and sighed and dropped to the ground.

清晨亲吻
夜的花朵
为时已晚，
她战栗
叹息着
凋落于地。

270

Through the sadness of all things I hear the crooning of the Eternal Mother.

从万物的忧伤之中
我听见了
永恒母亲的低吟。

271

I came to your shore as a stranger, I lived in your house
as a guest, I leave your door as a friend, my earth.

> 大地
> 初到你岸
> 我是生人，
> 住你家里
> 我是客人，
> 离开你家
> 我是友人。

272

Let my thoughts come to you, when I am gone, like the
after glow of sunset at the margin of starry silence.

> 当我离去，
> 让我的思绪走近你
> 如夕阳的余光
> 照在沉默的繁星边上。

273

Light in my heart the evening star of rest and then let
the night whisper to me of love.

> 在我心头
> 点燃安宁的夜星
> 好让黑夜向我
> 低诉爱情。

274

I am a child in the dark. I stretch my hands through the
coverlet of night for thee, Mother.

> 我是暗夜的孩子。
> 我从夜的帘幕里
> 向您伸出双手，
> 母亲。

275

The day of work is done. Hide my face in your arms,
Mother. Let me dream.

> 白天工作完成。
> 母亲，
> 请拥我入怀。
> 让我入梦。

276

The lamp of meeting burns long; it goes out in a
moment at the parting.

> 相聚时
> 灯光长明；
> 聚会一散
> 灯光便立刻熄灭。

277

One word keep for me in thy silence, O World, when I am dead, I have loved.

> 我死时，
> 世界，
> 请在沉默中为我留言，
> 我曾爱过。

278

We live in this world when we love it.

> 爱世界
> 才活在这世界。

279

Let the dead have the immortality of fame, but the living the immortality of love.

让逝者享有
永垂不朽的名声，
而让生者拥有
那不朽的爱情。

280

I have seen thee as the half-awakened child sees his mother in the dusk of the dawn and then smiles and sleeps again.

我看见你
犹如半醒的婴儿
在黎明晨曦中
看见母亲
而后微笑着
睡去。

281

I shall die again and again to know that life is inexhaustible.

我将一次次地死去
以确信生命的
永无止息。

282

While I was passing with the crowd in the road I saw
thy smile from the balcony and I sang and forgot all
noise.

随着人群走在路上
看见你在阳台微笑
我歌唱着
忘却了所有的喧嚣。

283

Love is life in its fulness like the cup with its wine.

爱是充盈的生命
像斟满的酒杯。

284

They light their own lamps and sing their own words in their temples. But the birds sing thy name in thine own morning light, —for thy name is joy.

> 他们在寺院亮灯
> 吟唱自己的话语。
> 小鸟在晨光中
> 唱着你的名字，
> 　——那就是快乐。

285

Lead me in the centre of thy silence to fill my heart with songs.

> 领我到你寂静中心
> 让我的心充满歌声。

286

Let them live who choose in their own hissing world of
fireworks. My heart longs for thy stars, my God.

让选焰火咝咝世界的人待在那。
我心渴望繁星，我的神。

287

Love's pain sang round my life like the unplumbed sea,
and love's joy sang like birds in its flowering groves.

爱之痛环绕我
如怒海歌唱，
爱之欢乐
如鸟儿在花丛歌唱。

288

Put out the lamp when thou wishest. I shall know thy darkness and shall love it.

> 如你愿意
> 就熄了灯。
> 我懂你的黑暗
> 也喜欢它。

289

When I stand before thee at the day's end thou shalt see my scars and know that I had my wounds and also my healing.

> 白天过去
> 我站在你面前
> 你将看到
> 我的伤疤
> 我的伤口
> 我在怎样疗伤。

290

Someday I shall sing to thee in the sunrise of some
other world, I have seen thee before in the light of
the earth, in the love of man.

> 有一天我将在
> 另一世界晨光里
> 唱颂你，
> 在地球的光里，
> 在人们的爱里，
> 我曾见过你。

291

Clouds come floating into my life from other days no
longer to shed rain or usher storm but to give colour to
my sunset sky.

> 从过去的日子
> 飘进我生命里的云彩
> 不再刮风下雨
> 而是为我夕阳的天空添彩。

292

Truth raises against itself the storm that scatters its
seeds broadcast.

真理促风雨反对自己
把真理种子散播。

293

The storm of the last night has crowned this morning
with golden peace.

昨夜
风雨以金色的宁静
给今晨
加冕。

294

Truth seems to come with its final word; and the final

word gives birth to its next.

> 真理似乎与结论同来;
> 结论孕育出下一个结论。

295

Blessed is he whose fame does not outshine his truth.

> 有福之人
> 名望未胜过真实。

296

Sweetness of thy name fills my heart when I forget mine—like thy morning sun when the mist is melted.

> 你的名字甜溢我心
> 我忘掉自己
> ——如早晨太阳升起
> 雾霾散去。

297

The silent night has the beauty of the mother and the
clamorous day of the child.

> 安静的夜
> 有母亲的丽质
> 喧闹的白天
> 有孩童的美丽。

298

The world loved man when he smiled. The world
became afraid of him when he laughed.

> 人微笑时
> 世界爱上他。
> 他大笑时
> 世界怕了他。

299

God waits for man to regain his childhood in wisdom.

> 神等待着人在智慧中
> 重获童年。

300

Let me feel this world as thy love taking form, then my love will help it.

> 让我感到世界
> 因你爱而成，
> 我的爱
> 将助它。

301

Thy sunshine smiles upon the winter days of my heart, never doubting of its spring flowers.

你的阳光
对我心中的冬天微笑，
从不疑它
春天的花朵。

302

God kisses the finite in his love and man the infinite.

神在爱里吻着有限
人却在吻着无限。

303

Thou crossest desert lands of barren years to reach the
moment of fulfilment.

越过荒芜之年的沙漠
你才能到达圆满的时刻。

304

God's silence ripens man's thoughts into speech.

神无言
使人思想成语言。

305

Thou wilt find, Eternal Traveller, marks of thy footsteps across my songs.

永恒行者，
你可在我的歌中
找寻到你的足迹。

306

Let me not shame thee, Father, who displayest thy glory in thy children.

不让您蒙羞，父亲，
您在孩子身上
展现出荣光。

307

Cheerless is the day, the light under frowning clouds is like a punished child with traces of tears on its pale cheeks, and the cry of the wind is like the cry of a wounded world. But I know I am travelling to meet my Friend.

阴郁的一天，
光在皱眉的云下
如被责罚的孩子
苍白脸上留着泪痕，
风在呼号
如一个受伤的世界的哭泣。
我知道我正在
跋涉去会友。

308

Tonight there is a stir among the palm leaves, a swell in the sea, Full Moon, like the heart-throb of the world. From what unknown sky hast thou carried in thy silence the aching secret of love?

今晚棕榈叶在摇动，
海上波涛汹涌，
满月啊，
如世界心脏搏动。
从哪个不可知的天空
你默默带来
爱的痛苦秘密？

309

I dream of a star, an island of light, where I shall be born and in the depth of its quickening leisure my life will ripen its works like the rice-field in the autumn sun.

我梦见
一颗星，
一座光之岛，
我将生在那里
在它高速悠闲深处
我的生命杰作
将要成熟
如秋阳下的稻地。

310

The smell of the wet earth in the rain rises like a great chant of praise from the voiceless multitude of the insignificant.

雨中湿润泥土气息升腾
如同从渺小无声的群众
那里传来的
宏大赞美歌声。

311

That love can ever lose is a fact that we cannot accept as truth.

> 爱会失去
> 这是事实
> 我们不肯
> 当真理接受。

312

We shall know some day that death can never rob us of that which our soul has gained, for her gains are one with herself.

> 我们终将明白
> 死永远无法夺去
> 我们灵魂所获,
> 其与灵魂已为一体。

313

God comes to me in the dusk of my evening with the flowers from my past kept fresh in his basket.

> 黄昏暮色中
> 神带着篮中还保鲜的
> 我的往日之花
> 来我这里。

314

When all the strings of my life will be tuned, my Master, then at every touch of thine will come out the music of love.

> 神啊，
> 当我生命琴弦
> 已调和谐，
> 你的每一次弹奏
> 都可以迸发出
> 爱的乐声。

315

Let me live truly, my Lord, so that death to me becomes true.

> 让我真实地生活，神啊，
> 死于我将成真。

316

Man's history is waiting in patience for the triumph of the insulted man.

> 人类历史
> 总是在耐心地等待着
> 被侮辱者的胜利。

317

I feel thy gaze upon my heart this moment like the

sunny silence of the morning upon the lonely field
whose harvest is over.

> 此刻我感到你眼光
> 正落在我心上
> 像那晨光中的沉默
> 落在收割后孤寂的田野上。

318

I long for the Island of Songs across this heaving Sea
of Shouts.

> 我渴望穿越
> 波涛汹涌的海
> 到达歌之岛。

319

The prelude of the night is commenced in the music of
the sunset, in its solemn hymn to the ineffable dark.

夜的序曲
始于夕阳西下的音乐，
始于向不可言喻的黑暗
所作的赞美诗。

320

I have scaled the peak and found no shelter in fame's bleak and barren height. Lead me, my Guide, before the light fades, into the valley of quiet where life's harvest mellows into golden wisdom.

登上峰顶我发现
荣誉的荒凉高处
无处栖身。
向导，
光明未逝前，
带我进入
一生收获将成熟为金色智慧的
宁静山谷。

321

Things look phantastic in this dimness of the dusk—
the spires whose bases are lost in the dark and tree-tops
like blots of ink. I shall wait for the morning and wake
up to see thy city in the light.

> 朦胧的暮色中
> 万物仿佛幻影——
> 尖塔底部在黑暗中消失
> 树冠如墨水模糊的斑点。
> 我等待黎明
> 醒来看到光明中
> 你的城市。

322

I have suffered and despaired and known death and I
am glad that I am in this great world.

经痛苦绝望
体味过死亡
我欣喜于活在
这伟大世界。

323

There are tracts in my life that are bare and silent. They
are the open spaces where my busy days had their light
and air.

我一生中有大片
空白与寂静。
它们是我忙碌时
获取阳光与空气的空地。

324

Release me from my unfulfilled past clinging to me
from behind making death difficult.

放了我吧
从后面缠绕我
使我难于死去的
未完成过去。

325

Let this be my last word, that I trust thy love.

相信你的爱，
这是我的结语。

莹火虫

Fireflies

（原著：[印]泰戈尔　黄建滨译）

Fireflies had their origin in China and Japan where thoughts were very often claimed from me in my handwriting on fans and pieces of silk.

Rabindranath Tagore

《萤火虫》源于中国和日本，
在那里我常应人之邀
把自己的所思所想
题写在扇子和丝绢上。

[印]拉宾德拉纳特·泰戈尔

1

My fancies are fireflies, — Specks of living light
twinkling in the dark.

> 我的幻想是萤火，
> ——生命的微光
> 黑暗中闪烁。

2

The voice of wayside pansies, that do not attract the
careless glance, murmurs in these desultory lines.

> 路边三色堇之声，
> 没有引起粗心人注意，
> 却在散乱诗句里
> 低语。

3

In the drowsy dark caves of the mind dreams build their nest with fragments dropped from day's caravan.

在沉寂黑暗的心洞
梦想
用白天商队遗留的碎片筑巢。

4

Spring scatters the petals of flowers that are not for the fruits of the future, but for the moment's whim.

春天吹落花瓣
不是为了将来的硕果，
而只是为了片刻的遐想。

5

Joy freed from the bond of earth's slumber rushes into

numberless leaves, and dances in the air for a day.

> 欢乐挣脱大地的睡梦
> 冲进无尽密叶之中,
> 从此终日
> 欢舞在空中。

6

My words that are slight may lightly dance upon time's
waves when my works heavy with import have gone
down.

> 我的短文
> 也许还在时间波浪上轻舞,
> 而我的鸿篇
> 却已沉没。

7

Mind's underground moths grow filmy wings and take
a farewell flight in the sunset sky.

心灵地下之蛾
长出薄翅
在日落空中
作告别飞行。

8

The butterfly counts not months but moments, and has time enough.

蝴蝶不计月份计瞬间，
因此时间充裕。

9

My thoughts, like sparks, ride on winged surprises, carrying a single laughter.

我思绪，
如星火，
载插翅惊异，
带纯朴微笑。

10

The tree gazes in love at its own beautiful shadow
which yet it never can grasp.

> 树木深情地凝视自己的倩影
> 却永远无法将它抓住。

11

Let my love, like sunlight, surround you and yet give
you illumined freedom.

> 让我的爱
> 如阳光围着你，
> 并赐你璀璨的自由。

12

Days are coloured bubbles that float upon the surface
of fathomless night.

白天是彩色的水泡
漂浮在深不可测的夜面。

13

My offerings are too timid to claim your remembrance,
and therefore you may remember them.

我的奉献
如此羞怯
不奢望你记住,
或许因此你铭记在心。

14

Leave out my name from the gift if it be a burden, but
keep my song.

名字是负担
从礼单抹去,
但请留下我的歌。

15

April, like a child, writes hieroglyphs on dust with flowers, wipes them away and forgets.

四月，像孩子，
用鲜花在土上
写象形文字，
抹去就忘记。

16

Memory, the priestess, kills the present and offers it heart to the shrine of the dead past.

记忆，是女祭司，
杀了现在，
用它的心祭奠
已逝旧日神龛。

17

From the solemn gloom of the temple children run out
to sit in the dust, God watches them play and forget the
priest.

孩子从庄严肃穆的庙宇跑出
坐在尘埃中，
神看他们玩
忘记了祭司。

18

My mind starts up at some flash on the flow of its
thoughts, like a brook at a sudden liquid note of its own
that is never repeated.

我的心在思想之流中
因刹那之光辉而惊动，
如小溪惊异于
永不重复的突兀音符。

19

In the mountain, stillness surges up to explore its own height; in the lake, movement stands still to contemplate its own depth.

> 在山里，寂静涌起
> 探测自己的高度；
> 在湖中，运动停下
> 沉思自己的深度。

20

The departing night's one kiss on the closed eyes of morning glows in the star of dawn.

> 将逝去的夜
> 对清晨紧闭双眼的吻
> 化作启明星光。

21

Maiden, thy beauty is like a fruit which is yet to mature,
tense with an unyielding secret.

少女啊，
你的美丽
如将成熟的果实，
因倔强的秘密而紧张。

22

Sorrow that has lost its memory is like the dumb dark
hours that have no bird songs, but only the cricket's
chirp.

失忆的忧愁
宛如喑哑黑暗的时刻，
没有了鸟儿歌唱，
只剩下蟋蟀唧唧。

23

Bigotry tries to keep truth safe in its hand with a grip
that kill it.

Wishing to hearten a timid lamp great night lights all
her stars.

> 偏执竭力想把真理
> 握在手心
> 却将它扼杀。
> 伟夜想鼓励害羞的灯
> 却点亮满天星。

24

Though he holds in his arms the earth-bride, the sky is
ever immensely away.

> 天空虽把大地新娘拥怀中，
> 但两者依然很遥远。

25

God seeks comrades and claims love, the devil seeks slaves and claims obedience.

> 神觅同伴索爱，
> 魔鬼寻找奴仆
> 并令其臣服。

26

The soil in return for her service keeps the tree tied to her, the sky asks nothing and leaves it free.

> 泥土把树绑在身上
> 作为养育的回报，
> 天空无所求
> 任其自由。

27

Jewel-like the immortal does not boast of its length of years but of the scintillating point of its moment.

宝石如不朽者
夸耀的并非它悠久的历史
而是耀眼于瞬间的光芒。

28

The child ever dwells in the mystery of ageless time, unobscured by the dust of history.

孩子总是居住在永恒的神秘之中，
不会受到历史尘埃蒙蔽。

29

A light laughter in the steps of creation carries it swiftly across time.

创造步履中的一声浅笑
带着它
瞬间跨越时空。

30

One who was distant came near to me in the morning,
and still nearer when taken away by night.

清晨那个遥远的人
向我走过来，
黑夜将他带走
却离我更近。

31

White and pink oleanders meet and make merry in
different dialects.

粉白夹竹桃相遇
用不同方言
快乐地交谈。

32

When peace is active sweeping its dirt, it is storm.

> 和平奋力荡涤污垢，
> 就是风暴。

33

The lake lies low by the hill, a tearful entreaty of love at the foot of the inflexible.

> 湖泊低卧于山边，
> 在铁石心肠者的足下
> 泪水涟涟
> 向其示爱。

34

There smiles the Divine Child among his playthings of unmeaning clouds and ephemeral lights and shadows.

圣子
在索然无味的云彩
与瞬息万变的光和阴影中
展露笑颜。

35

The breeze whispers to the lotus, "What is thy secret?"
"It is myself," says the lotus, "steal it and I disappear!"

微风对莲花低语：
"你有什么秘密？"
莲花答道：
"是我自己，
偷了它我即消失！"

36

The freedom of the storm and the bondage of the stem
join hands in the dance of swaying branches.

暴风雨的自由
和树干的束缚携手
在摇曳的树枝中跳舞。

37

The jasmine's lisping of love to the sun is her flowers.

茉莉对太阳示爱的呢喃
是她的花。

38

The tyrant claims freedom to kill freedom and yet to keep it for himself.

暴君宣扬自由
是为了杀它
却把它留给自己。

39

Gods, tired of their paradise, envy man.

> 诸神，
> 厌倦了天堂，
> 羡慕凡间。

40

Clouds are hills in vapour, hills are clouds in stone, —a phantasy in time's dream.

> 云是水汽之山，
> 山是石之云，
> ——时间之梦的幻象。

41

While God waits for His temple to be built of love, men bring stones.

神期待以爱筑庙宇，
人们带来了石头。

42

I touch God in my song as the hill touches the far-away
sea with its waterfall.

我用歌声感动神
正如大山用瀑布
感动远方的海洋。

43

Light finds her treasure of colours through the
antagonism of clouds.

在与云的抗衡中
光找到她多彩的宝藏。

44

My heart to-day smiles at its past night of tears like a wet tree glistening in the sun after the rain is over.

> 我今日之心
> 笑对流泪的昨夜
> 如雨后在阳光下
> 闪闪发光的潮湿大树。

45

I have thanked the trees that have made my life fruitful, but have failed to remember the grass that has ever kept it green.

> 我感谢大树
> 是它使我生命硕果累累，
> 却忘了小草
> 是它使我生命常青。

46

The one without second is emptiness, the other one makes it true.

> 有一无二只是空空如也，
> 一因有二才真实。

47

Life's errors cry for the merciful beauty that can modulate their isolation into a harmony with the whole.

> 生命中的错误
> 泣求慈悲的美
> 以调和它们的孤寂
> 达到与整体的和谐统一。

48

They expect thanks for the banished nest because their

cage is shapely and secure.

他们期望因捣毁鸟巢获赞
因为鸟笼牢固美观。

49

In love I pay my endless debt to thee for what thou art.

不论你怎样
我用爱还你无穷债款。

50

The pond sends up its lyrics from its dark in lilies, and
the sun says, they are good.

池塘献上百合暗丛中的抒情诗，
太阳说，
它们真好。

51

Your calumny against the great is impious, it hurts yourself; against the small it is mean, for it hurts the victim.

> 诽谤伟人
> 你毫无敬意,
> 伤害了自己;
> 诽谤小人物
> 你卑鄙,
> 伤害了牺牲者。

52

The first flower that blossomed on this earth was an invitation to the unborn song.

> 这星球开放的第一朵花
> 是发给未出世之歌的请柬。

53

Dawn—the many-coloured flower—fades, and then
the simple light-fruit, the sun appears.

拂晓——
多彩的花——
谢去，
那单纯的果实，
太阳
冉冉升起。

54

The muscle that has a doubt of its wisdom throttles the
voice that would cry.

肌肉怀疑自己的智慧
因而扼杀了哭叫之声。

55

The wind tries to take the flame by storm only to blow it out.

风企图用暴雨攫取火苗
却将其熄灭。

56

Life's play is swift. Life's playthings fall behind one by one and are forgotten.

人生游戏
快速地收场。
人生玩具
被逐个遗忘。

57

My flower, seek not thy paradise in a fool's buttonhole.

我的花，
别在蠢人扣眼里
觅你的天堂。

58

Thou hast risen late, my crescent moon, but my night
bird is still awake to greet thee.

我的新月，
你姗姗来迟，
我的夜鸟未睡
等着问候你。

59

Darkness is the veiled bride silently waiting for the
errant light to return to her bosom.

黑夜是披纱的新娘
静静地等待漫游的光明
重回她怀抱。

60

Trees are the earth's endless effort to speak to the listening heaven.

> 树木是大地
> 对谛听的天空
> 无休止的诉说。

61

The burden of self is lightened when I laugh at myself.

> 当我自嘲时
> 自私的负担随之减轻。

62

The weak can be terrible because they try furiously to appear strong.

弱小者也会令人害怕，
因他们切盼显得强大。

63

The wind of heaven blows, the anchor desperately clutches the mud, and my boat is beating its breast against the chain.

天堂的风刮起，
锚拼命地抓紧淤泥，
我的小船
用自己的胸膛
撞击着铁链。

64

The spirit of death is one, the spirit of life is many. When God is dead religion becomes one.

死亡精灵唯一，
生命精灵形式多种。

当神死去时，
宗教合而为一。

65

The blue of the sky longs for the earth's green, the
wind between them sighs, "Alas."

蔚蓝天空渴盼大地碧绿，
"唉!" 风在天地间哀叹。

66

Day's pain muffled by its own glare, burns among stars
in the night.

昼痛被自身光所蔽，
却在夜星中燃烧。

67

The stars crowd round the virgin night in silent awe at
her loneliness that can never be touched.

群星簇拥着处子之夜
敬畏地静望着
她永难触及的孤独。

68

The cloud gives all its gold to the departing sun and
greets the rising moon with only a pale smile.

云给离去的太阳
以全部黄金
用苍白微笑
向初升月亮致意。

69

He who does good comes to the temple gate, he who loves reaches the shrine.

行善者只来到大庙门口，
博爱者进到殿堂。

70

Flower, have pity for the worm, it is not a bee, its love is a blunder and burden.

花啊，
可怜这小虫吧，
它不是蜜蜂，
它的爱是大错和负担。

71

With the ruins of terror's triumph children build

their doll's house.

孩子用恐怖胜利残片
建造玩偶之家。

72

The lamp waits through the long day of neglect for the
flame's kiss in the night.

灯熬过漫长冷漠白天
等待夜晚火焰亲吻。

73

Feathers in the dust lying lazily content have forgotten
their sky.

羽毛慵懒躺在尘埃里
心满意足
忘记了天空。

74

The flower which is single need not envy the thorns
that are numerous.

> 孤单的花朵
> 没有必要妒忌
> 那数不清的荆棘。

75

The world suffers most from the disinterested tyranny
of its well-wisher.

> 世界因好心人公正的专横
> 而蒙受极大的痛楚。

76

We gain freedom when we have paid the full price for
our right to live.

我们为生存权
付出全部代价
赢下自由。

77

Your careless gifts of a moment, like the meteors of an autumn night, catch fire the depth of my being.

你刹那间漫不经心的礼物，
如秋夜的彗星，
点亮我生命
深处的火。

78

The faith waiting in the heart of a seed promises a miracle of life which it cannot prove at once.

信仰
静待在种子的心中

预示着一个无法立刻验证的
生命奇迹。

79

Spring hesitates at winter's door, but the mango blossom
rashly runs out to him before her time and meets her doom.

> 春
> 在冬天门前犹豫，
> 但杧果花冒冒失失
> 向他奔去
> 花期未到
> 遭遇厄运。

80

The world is the ever-changing foam that floats on the
surface of a sea of silence.

> 世界是变化无常的泡沫，
> 漂浮在寂静的大海之中。

81

The two separated shores mingle their voices in a song
of unfathomed tears.

> 彼此分开的两岸的歌声
> 在深不可测的泪中融合。

82

As a river in the sea, work finds its fulfillment in the
depth of leisure.

> 犹如江河汇入大海，
> 工作在闲暇深处
> 获得完满。

83

I lingered on my way till thy cherry tree lost its blossom,
but the azalea brings to me, my love, thy forgiveness.

我在路上徘徊不前
直到樱桃树花落，
我的爱啊，
杜鹃花送来了，
你的宽恕。

84

Thy shy little pomegranate bud, blushing to-day behind her veil, will burst into a passionate flower to-morrow when I am away.

今天娇羞的小石榴花蕾
在面纱后羞红脸，
明天当我离去
你却会绽放
热情洋溢的花朵。

85

The clumsiness of power spoils the key, and uses the pickaxe.

权力笨拙地宠坏了钥匙，
竟用起鹤嘴锄。

86

Birth is from the mystery of night into the greater mystery of day.

诞生来自黑夜的神秘
进到更大的白昼神秘中。

87

These paper boats of mine are meant to dance on the ripples of hours, and not to reach any destination.

我这些纸船
只愿在时光涟漪上
翩翩起舞，
却不想抵达
任何目的地。

88

Migratory songs wing from my heart and seek their nests in your voice of love.

流浪的歌飞出我心头
在你爱的呼唤中觅巢。

89

The sea of danger, doubt and denial around man's little island of certainty challenges him to dare the unknown.

危险、疑问和否定的汪洋大海
围着人类执念的小小岛屿
催他向未知挑战。

90

Love punishes when it forgives, and injured beauty by its awful silence.

爱情宽恕
便是惩罚，
还用可怕的沉默
伤害了美。

91

You live alone and unrecompensed because they are afraid of your great worth.

你生活孤单从未得报
因他们害怕你伟大价值。

92

The same sun is newly born in new lands in a ring of endless dawns.

无尽的黎明环中
同一旭日在新地上重生。

93

God's world is ever renewed by death, a Titan's ever crushed by its own existence.

> 神界因死亡而重生，
> 泰坦永远被其自身存在碾碎。

94

The glow-worm while exploring the dust never knows that stars are in the sky.

> 萤火虫在泥土中摸索，
> 从不知道有星星满天。

95

The tree is of to-day, the flower is old, it brings with it the message of the immemorial seed.

树是今天的，
花儿却很古老，
它带来太古洪荒时
种子的消息。

96

Each rose that comes brings me greetings from the Rose of an eternal spring.

每朵玫瑰都带给我
永恒春天玫瑰的祝福。

97

God honours me when I work, He loves me when I sing.

我工作时神敬我，
歌唱时他爱我。

98

My love of to-day finds no home in the nest deserted
by yesterday's love.

在昨天爱遗弃了的窠里
我今天的爱找不到家。

99

The fire of pain traces for my soul a luminous path
across her sorrow.

痛苦的火经她的忧郁
替我心灵探到一光明之路。

100

The grass survives the hill through its resurrections
from countless deaths.

草从无数死亡中复活
所以它比山长寿。

101

Thou hast vanished from my reach leaving an impalpable touch in the blue of the sky, an invisible image in the wind moving among the shadows.

你从我手中
消失在蔚蓝天空
留下感觉不到的一触，
一个在风中飘摇在影子里
不可见的幻象。

102

In pity for the desolate branch spring leaves to it a kiss that fluttered in a lonely leaf.

为怜惜凄凉的树枝
春天留给它
在孤叶里振动过的吻。

103

The shy shadow in the garden loves the sun in silence,
Flowers guess the secret, and smile, while the leaves
whisper.

花园里羞涩的暗影
默默爱着太阳，
花猜透秘密，微笑，
树叶窃窃私语。

104

I leave no trace of wings in the air, but I am glad I have
had my flight.

我没在空中留下翅痕，
但我高兴我曾经飞翔。

105

The fireflies, twinkling among leaves, make the stars wonder.

> 绿叶间萤火闪闪，
> 使繁星为之惊叹。

106

The mountain remains unmoved at its seeming defeat by the mist.

> 云雾仿佛击败大山
> 大山依旧岿然不动。

107

While the rose said to the sun, "I shall ever remember thee," her pedals fell to the dust.

正当玫瑰对太阳说，
"我会永远记住你，"
她的花瓣已入土。

108

Hills are the earth's gesture of despair for the unreachable.

高山是大地
对难及之地的
绝望姿势。

109

Though the thorn in thy flower pricked me, O Beauty, I am grateful.

你的荆棘虽刺痛我，
噢，美人，
我仍感激你。

110

The world knows that the few are more than the many.

> 世界知道
> 少数比多数更强大。

111

Let not my love be a burden on you, my friend, know
that it pays itself.

> 别让我的爱
> 成为你负担,
> 朋友,
> 要知道它值得。

112

Dawn plays her lute before the gate of darkness, and is
content to vanish when the sun comes out.

黎明在黑暗门前
弹起琴弦，
太阳出来
便心满意足地离去。

113

Beauty is truth's smile when she beholds her own face
in a perfect mirror.

美是真的微笑
当她在完美镜中
看自己的脸。

114

The dew-drop knows the sun only within its own tiny orb.

露珠
只是在自己的小球里
认识太阳。

115

Forlorn thoughts from the forsaken hives of all ages,
swarming in the air, hum round my heart and seek my
voice.

被弃的思想
从世代废弃蜂巢飞出，
遍布空中，
围着我心
求我发声。

116

The desert is imprisoned in the wall of its unbounded
barrenness.

沙漠被囚禁
在自己无边无际的
荒芜的墙里。

117

In the thrill of little leaves I see the air's invisible dance, and in their glimmering the secret heart-beats of the sky.

> 从小小树叶颤动
> 我看到空气无形之舞，
> 从其闪闪微光
> 看到天空秘密心跳。

118

You are like a flowering tree, amazed when I praise you for your gifts.

> 你像棵开花的大树，
> 惊异于我赞美你天赋。

119

The earth's sacrificial fire flames up in her trees,
scattering sparks in flowers.

> 大地的祭火
> 在树林中燃起，
> 火星四散
> 溅落成花。

120

Forests, the clouds of earth, hold up to the sky their
silence, and clouds from above come down in resonant
showers.

> 森林，
> 大地的云朵，
> 把寂静献给天空，
> 云朵
> 从天空降落
> 化作阵雨唱和。

121

The world speaks to me in pictures, my soul answers in music.

世界用图和我对话，
我灵魂以乐作答。

122

The sky tells its beads all night on the countless stars in memory of the sun.

碧空整夜数着
无数繁星串成的念珠
缅怀太阳。

123

The darkness of night, like pain, is dumb, the darkness of dawn, like peace, is silent.

夜晚黑暗
如痛苦喑哑，
黎明黑暗
如和平寂静。

124

Pride engraves his frowns in stones, love offers her surrender in flowers.

傲慢刻皱眉于石中，
爱情用鲜花表示投降。

125

The obsequious brush curtails truth in deference to the canvas which is narrow.

谄媚的画笔
压缩真实的图景
屈从于狭窄的画布。

126

The hill in its longing for the far-away sky wishes to be like the cloud with its endless urge of seeking.

> 高山仰慕
> 遥远的天空
> 希望自己像云彩一样
> 拥有无尽追求的冲动。

127

To justify their own spilling of ink they spell the day as night.

> 为证明泼墨有理
> 他们把白天说成黑夜。

128

Profit smiles on goodness when the good is profitable.

善举有利可图时
利益对善举微笑。

129

In its swelling pride the bubble doubts the truth of the sea, and laughs and bursts into emptiness.

泡沫自负膨胀
怀疑起大海的真实，
因大笑爆裂
化为虚无。

130

Love is an endless mystery, for it has nothing else to explain it.

爱情是无尽的奥秘，
因任何事物都无法释义。

131

My clouds, sorrowing in the dark, forget that they themselves have hidden the sun.

> 我的云在黑暗中悲伤，
> 忘记是他们遮蔽了太阳。

132

Man discovers his own wealth when God comes to ask gifts of him.

> 神索礼之时
> 人们才发现
> 自己的财富。

133

You have your memory as a flame to my lonely lamp of separation.

你把你火焰般的回忆
留给了我那分离的孤灯。

134

I came to offer thee a flower, but thou must have all my
garden, it is thine.

我来献给你一朵花，
可你却要我整座花园，
拿去吧。

135

The picture——a memory of light treasured by the
shadow.

图画——
是阴影所珍藏的
一幅光的回忆。

136

It is easy to make faces at the sun,
He is exposed by his own light in all directions.

> 对太阳做鬼脸容易，
> 因他从四面八方
> 暴露在自己的光芒中。

137

Love remains a secret when spoken, for only a lover
truly knows he is loved.

> 爱情说出
> 依然是秘密，
> 因为只有爱人知道
> 自己被爱。

138

History slowly smothers its truth, but hastily struggles to revive it in the terrible penance of pain.

> 历史慢慢扼杀
> 自身真相，
> 在可怕痛苦的悔过中
> 又匆匆费力重现真相。

139

My work is rewarded in daily wages, I wait for my final value in love.

> 我的工作
> 每日都有薪酬，
> 就盼在爱中
> 实现最终价值。

140

Beauty knows to say, "Enough," barbarism clamours for still more.

美懂得说："够了。"
粗俗却吵闹着要更多。

141

God loves to see in me not his servant, but himself who serves all.

神乐见
我不是仆人，
而是服务众人的他。

142

The darkness of night is in harmony with day, the morning of mist is discordant.

夜晚的黑暗和白天
和谐一致，
有雾的早晨
并不和谐。

143

In the bounteous time of roses love is wine, —it is food in the famished hour when their petals are shed.

玫瑰丰裕的时节
爱情是酒，
——饥饿时节
花瓣凋谢脱落
就成了食物。

144

An unknown flower in a strange land speaks to the poet: "Are we not of the same soil, my lover?"

陌生土地的无名花朵
对诗人说：
"我的情人，
咱们莫非是同乡？"

145

I am able to love my God because He gives me
freedom to deny Him.

我能够爱我的神
因为神给了我
否定他的自由。

146

My untuned strings beg for music in their anguished
cry of shame.

羞愧痛苦声中
走调的琴弦
乞求音乐。

147

The worm thinks it strange and foolish that man does
not eat his books.

> 人不吃他的书
> 蛀虫认为这怪且愚蠢。

148

The clouded sky to-day bears the vision of the shadow
of a divine sadness on the forehead of brooding
eternity.

> 乌云密布的今天
> 在沉思默想的永恒的额头上
> 拥有神圣悲伤的
> 阴影景象。

149

The shade of my tree is for passers-by, its fruit for the
one for whom I wait.

我的树荫是为了路人的，
而果实留给我等待的人。

150

Flushed with the glow of sunset earth seems like a ripe
fruit ready to be harvested by night.

夕阳辉映的大地
满面红晕
如熟透果实
等夜晚收获。

151

Light accepts darkness for his spouse for the sake of creation.

> 为了天地万物
> 光明接受黑暗为配偶。

152

The reed waits for his master's breath, the Master goes seeking for his reed.

> 芦笛等待主人气息，
> 主人找寻自己的芦笛。

153

To the blind pen the hand that writes is unreal, its writing unmeaning.

盲笔认为写字的手不真实，
所写毫无意义。

154

The sea smites his own barren breast because he has no
flowers to offer to the moon.

> 大海捶打自己
> 荒芜的胸膛
> 因他没有鲜花
> 献给月亮。

155

The greed for fruit misses the flower.

> 贪图果实
> 却失去花朵。

156

God in His temple of stars waits for man to bring him
his lamp.

在繁星圣殿里的神
等待着凡人献灯。

157

The fire restrained in the tree fashions flowers.
Released from bonds, the shameless flame dies in
barren ashes.

被困树中之火
塑造花朵。
无耻的火
摆脱束缚，
死于贫瘠灰烬。

158

The sky sets no snare to capture the moon, it is her own freedom which binds her. The light that fills the sky seeks its limit in a dew-drop on the grass.

> 天空没有设网捕捉月亮，
> 月亮的自由束缚了她。
> 充满天空的光
> 在草地的露珠里
> 寻求极限。

159

Wealth is the burden of bigness, welfare the fulness of being.

> 财富是显摆的负担，
> 幸福是生命的丰满。

160

The razor-blade is proud of its keenness when it sneers at the sun.

　　剃刀之刃以锋利骄傲
　　竟嘲笑起了太阳。

161

The butterfly has leisure to love the lotus, not the bee busily storing honey.

　　五彩蝴蝶有闲暇
　　去爱恋莲花，
　　蜜蜂忙着储蜜
　　无此闲暇。

162

Child, thou bringest to my heart the babble of the wind
and the water, the flower's speechless secrets, the cloud's
dreams, the mute gaze of wonder of the morning sky.

> 孩子，
> 你给我的心带来风的呼号，
> 潺潺水声，
> 鲜花无言的秘密，
> 云的梦想
> 和晨空惊奇的
> 默默注视。

163

The rainbow among the clouds may be great but the
little butterfly among the bushes is greater.

> 云间的彩虹
> 也许很伟大
> 但是灌木丛中的小小蝴蝶
> 更加不凡。

164

The mist weaves her net round the morning, captivates
him, and makes him blind.

> 雾霭在清晨
> 编织罗网，
> 迷住黎明，
> 使他目盲。

165

The Morning Star whispers to Dawn, "Tell me that you
are only for me." "Yes," she answers. "And also only
for that nameless flower."

> 晨星对黎明低语，
> "告诉我你只是为了我。"
> "是，"她回答，
> "也只是为了那
> 无名的花朵。"

166

The sky remains infinitely vacant for earth there to build its heaven with dreams.

> 天空始终保持
> 无限空旷
> 以便大地用梦
> 建造天堂。

167

Perhaps the crescent moon smiles in doubt at being told that it is a fragment awaiting perfection.

> 听说自己是等待圆满的残片
> 新月也许会露出
> 质疑的微笑。

168

Let the evening forgive the mistakes of the day and thus win peace for herself.

让黄昏原谅白天的错误
从而为自己赢得安宁。

169

Beauty smiles in the confinement of the bud, in the heart of a sweet incompleteness.

在甜蜜的尚未圆满的心中，
受困于蓓蕾
美微微一笑。

170

Your flitting love lightly brushed with its wings my sunflower and never asked if it was ready to surrender its honey.

你的爱一掠而过
用翅膀轻拂我的向日葵
却从不问它是否准备
献上花蜜。

171

Leaves are silences around flowers which are their words.

叶静静围绕着花，
花是叶的语言。

172

The tree bears its thousand years as one large majestic moment.

树将其千年岁月
化为一个壮丽时刻。

173

My offerings are not for the temple at the end of the road, but for the wayside shrines that surprise me at every bend.

> 我的供奉不为
> 设在道路尽头的神殿，
> 而为途中每个拐角处
> 给我惊喜的神龛。

174

Your smile, my love, like the smell of a strange flower, is simple and inexplicable.

> 我的爱，
> 你微笑如奇花的芳香，
> 那么单纯
> 却令人费解。

175

Death laughs when the merit of the dead is exaggerated
for it swells his store with more than he can claim.

死亡的美德被夸大
死神哈哈笑
膨胀的库房
超出其拥有的容量。

176

The sigh of the shore follows in vain the breeze that
hastens the ship across the sea.

海岸叹息着
徒劳追随
催赶船儿穿越大海的
微风。

177

Truth loves its limits, for there it meets the beautiful.

> 真理爱其边界，
> 因在那里遇到美。

178

Between the shores of Me and Thee there is the loud ocean, my own surging self, which I long to cross.

> 你我的两岸之间
> 隔着喧嚣海洋，
> 汹涌的自我，
> 我渴望渡过。

179

The right to possess boasts foolishly of its right to enjoy.

占有的权利
愚蠢夸耀
它享有的权利。

180

The rose is a great deal more than a blushing apology
for the thorn.

玫瑰远非为她的荆棘
而表示的羞红的歉意。

181

Day offers to the silence of stars his golden lute to be
tuned for the endless life.

白天献给沉默的繁星
他的金琴
为永恒的生命定音。

182

The wise know how to teach, the fool how to smite.

> 智者知如何教,
> 愚者知责打。

183

The centre is still and silent in the heart of an eternal dance of circles.

> 在永恒不停的
> 环舞的核心区
> 中间位置
> 静止无声。

184

The judge thinks that he is just when he compares the oil of another's lamp with the light of his own.

法官把其他人的灯油
与自己的灯光相比,
以为自己很公正。

185

The captive flower in the King's wreath smiles bitterly
when the meadow-flower envies her.

国王花冠上
被囚的花
对羡慕她的草地之花
露出苦笑。

186

Its store of snow is the hill's own burden, its
outpouring of streams is borne by all the world.

积雪是大山
自己的负担,

它奔泻的溪流
整个世界承担。

187

Listen to the prayer of the forest for its freedom in
flowers.

听
森林在为其鲜花的自由绽放
发出祈祷。

188

Let your love see me even through the barrier of
nearness.

让你的爱
透过亲近的栅栏
看看我。

189

The spirit of work in creation is there to carry and help the spirit of play.

> 创造中的工作精神
> 只是为了保持
> 并帮助游乐之魂。

190

To carry the burden of the instrument, count the cost of its material, and never to know that it is for music, is the tragedy of deaf life.

> 承载着乐器的重负，
> 算计着材料的支出，
> 始终不知
> 它是为了音乐而生，
> 这才是聋人生活的
> 悲剧。

191

Faith is the bird that feels the light and sings when the dawn is still dark.

信仰
是黎明暗黑中
感觉到光
唱歌的鸟。

192

I bring to thee, night, my day's empty cup, to be cleansed with thy cool darkness for a new morning's festival.

黑夜，
我给你白昼的空杯，
用你凉爽黑暗清洗，
迎接早晨全新节日。

193

The mountain fir, in its rustling, modulates the memory
of its fights with the storm into a hymn of peace.

> 沙沙作响的
> 高山冷杉
> 把它与暴风雨搏斗的记忆
> 谱成了和平颂歌。

194

God honoured me with his fight when I was rebellious,
He ignored me when I was languid.

> 当我反抗时
> 神赐我战斗荣耀，
> 当我颓丧时
> 他不理不睬。

195

The sectarian thinks that he has the sea ladled into his private pond.

> 偏执狂以为
> 他已将大海
> 舀进他的
> 私家池塘。

196

In the shady depth of life are the lonely nests of memories that shrink from words.

> 记忆的孤单之巢
> 躲着言语
> 藏在生命的
> 阴暗深处。

197

Let my love find its strength in the service of day, its peace in the union of night.

让我的爱
服务白天
找到力量，
联合黑夜
找到安宁。

198

Life sends up in blades of grass its silent hymn of praise to the unnamed Light.

生命
用片片草叶
向无名之光献上
无声赞歌。

199

The stars of night are to me the memorials of my day's faded flowers.

> 夜晚繁星对于我
> 是对白昼凋谢之花的
> 纪念。

200

Open thy door to that which must go, for the loss becomes unseemly when obstructed.

> 打开门
> 要走的由它去，
> 因为阻拦蒙受损失
> 毫无意义。

201

True end is not in the reaching of the limit, but in a
completion which is limitless.

真正的终点
不是到达极限，
而是在于成就
无限的圆满。

202

The shore whispers to the sea: "Write to me what thy
waves struggle to say."
The sea writes in foam again and again and wipes off
lines in a boisterous despair.

海岸对大海低语：
"写下波浪拼命想说的话。"
大海用泡沫反复书写
又在狂暴的绝望中
逐行删除。

203

Let the touch of thy finger thrill my life's strings and make the music thine and mine.

让你的手指
拨动我生命琴弦
奏出你我的音乐。

204

The inner world rounded in my life like a fruit, matured in joy and sorrow, will drop into the darkness of the original soil for some further course of creation.

我生活的内心世界
圆如果实，
在悲与喜中成熟，
为了进一步的创造过程
将叶落归根在故土的
黑暗之中。

205

Form is in Matter, rhythm in Force, meaning in the Person.

> 形式物显示，
> 韵律力控制，
> 意义人诠释。

206

There are seekers of wisdom and seekers of wealth, I seek thy company so that I may sing.

> 有人寻求智慧
> 有人追求财富，
> 我求你相伴
> 让我放声歌唱。

207

As the tree its leaves, I shed my words on the earth, let
my thoughts unuttered flower in thy silence.

> 如大树落叶，
> 我撒言语在大地，
> 让我未说之思
> 开在你沉默里。

208

My faith in truth, my vision of the perfect, help thee,
Master, in thy creation.

> 神啊，
> 让我对真理的信仰，
> 对完美的想象，
> 助你创世。

209

All the delights that I have felt in life's fruits and flowers let me offer to thee at the end of the feast, in a perfect union of love.

> 在盛宴结束之时，
> 让我把人生的花与果中的一切欢乐
> 融于圆满结合的爱
> 奉献给你。

210

Some have thought deeply and explored the meaning of thy truth, and they are great; I have listened to catch the music of thy play, and I am glad.

> 有人深思熟虑
> 探求你真理的意义，
> 他们伟大；
> 我凝神谛听
> 捕捉你演奏的乐曲，
> 心欢畅。

211

The tree is a winged spirit released from the bondage of seed, pursuing its adventure of life across the unknown.

大树是摆脱了
种子束缚的
带翅精灵，
穿越未知世界
追寻生命探险之旅。

212

The lotus offers its beauty to the heaven, the grass its service to the earth.

莲花把自己的美
奉献给天空，
绿草则是
服务大地。

213

The sun's kiss mellows into abandonment the miserliness of the green fruit clinging to its stem.

> 太阳的亲吻
> 催熟依附于树枝的
> 吝啬青涩之果
> 使之无拘无束。

214

The flame met the earthen lamp in me, and what a great marvel of light!

> 火焰遇到我心中的陶灯，
> 多么神奇的光明！

215

Mistakes live in the neighbourhood of truth and therefore delude us.

> 错误是真理的邻居
> 我们因此而被欺骗。

216

The cloud laughed at the rainbow saying that it was an upstart gaudy in its emptiness.

The rainbow calmly answered, "I am as inevitably real as the sun himself."

> 云朵嘲笑彩虹
> 说它是个空洞无物
> 华而不实的暴发户。
> 彩虹平静地回答：
> 　"我像太阳本身一样真实
> 毋庸置疑。"

217

Let me not grope in vain in the dark but keep my mind still in the faith that the day will break and truth will appear in its simplicity.

> 不要让我在黑暗中
> 徒劳摸索
> 要让我毫不动摇地坚信
> 天将破晓
> 真理将显露纯真。

218

Through the silent night I hear the returning vagrant hopes of the morning knock at my heart.

> 透过无声的夜
> 我听见
> 回归漂泊晨的希望
> 叩响我心房。

219

My new love comes bringing to me the eternal wealth
of the old.

> 新的爱情带来
> 曾经的爱情的
> 永恒财富。

220

The earth gazes at the moon and wonders that she
should have all her music in her smile.

> 大地凝视月亮
> 惊叹
> 她把她所有的音乐
> 都融进微笑。

221

Day with its glare of curiosity puts the stars to flight.

> 白天好奇的瞪视
> 吓得繁星
> 惊慌离去。

222

My mind has its true union with thee, O sky, at the window which is mine own, and not in the open where thou hast thy sole kingdom.

> 天空啊,
> 我的心真正与你交融,
> 在我自己的窗口,
> 而不是在你专属的
> 王国的旷野。

223

Man claims God's flowers as his own when he weaves them in a garland.

> 人把神的花
> 编织成花环
> 声称
> 花属于他。

224

The buried city, laid bare to the sun of a new age, is ashamed that it has lost all its songs.

> 被埋的城市，
> 在新时代
> 重见天日，
> 因它的歌遗失
> 而感到羞愧。

225

Like my heart's pain that has long missed its meaning,
the sun's rays robed in dark hide themselves under the
ground.

Like my heart's pain at love's sudden touch, they
change their veil at the spring's call and come out in
the carnival of colours, in flowers and leaves.

> 如我早已失去意义的心痛，
> 太阳光线穿着黑袍
> 藏在地下。
> 如我被爱突然触动的心痛，
> 听春天召唤它们
> 换了面纱，
> 在花叶色彩狂欢中
> 登场。

226

My life's empty flute waits for its final music like the
primal darkness before the stars came out.

我生命空寂的长笛
等待着终曲
如繁星出现前
最初的黑暗。

227

Emancipation from the bondage of the soil is no freedom for the tree.

从泥土束缚中
获得解放
对树木而言
并非自由。

228

The tapestry of life's story is woven with the threads of life's ties ever joining and breaking.

人生故事的挂毯
是由人生不断时合时断之线
编织而成。

229

Those thoughts of mine that are never captured by words perch upon my songs and dances.

我那些从未被文字俘获的思想
栖息在歌舞之上。

230

My soul to-night loses itself in the silent heart of a tree standing alone among the whispers of immensity.

今夜我的灵魂
遗失在一棵树沉默的心里
树孤独地站在
巨量的低语之中。

231

Pearl shells cast up by the sea on death's barren beach,
—a magnificent wastefulness of creative life.

> 大海把珍珠壳
> 抛向死亡荒芜海滩，
> ——这是生命创造的
> 壮观浪费。

232

The sunlight opens for me the world's gate, love's light
its treasure.

> 阳光为我开世界之门，
> 爱之光开宝库。

233

My life like the reed with its stops, has its play of

colours through the gaps in its hopes and gains.

> 我的人生
> 如多孔芦笛，
> 穿过希望与收获孔隙
> 奏出多彩。

234

Let not my thanks to thee rob my silence of its fuller homage.

> 别让我的感激
> 剥夺我缄默对你的敬意。

235

Life's aspirations come in the guise of children.

> 生命的志向
> 装扮成孩童出场。

236

The faded flower sighs that the spring has vanished for
ever.

凋零的花朵哀叹
春天已去
不再回返。

237

In my life's garden my wealth has been of the shadows
and lights that are never gathered and stored.

在我人生的花园中
我的财富
是从未收集贮藏的
光与影。

238

The fruit that I have gained for ever is that which thou hast accepted.

> 我所永久收获的果实
> 就是你接受的果实。

239

The jasmine knows the sun to be her brother in the heaven.

> 茉莉花知道
> 太阳是她在天上的兄长。

240

Light is young, the ancient light; shadows are of the moment, they are born old.

光年轻，
地老天荒；
阴影只不过片刻，
出生即老。

241

I feel that the ferry of my songs at the day's end will bring me across to the other shore from where I shall see.

我感到我的歌声的渡船
在白日将尽之时
将把我载到彼岸
远眺观望。

242

The butterfly flitting from flower to flower ever remains mine, I lose the one that is netted by me.

在花朵之间
飞来飞去的蝴蝶
永远属于我,
被我网住的
我却失去了。

243

Your voice, free bird, reaches my sleeping nest, and my
drowsy wings dream of a voyage to the light above the
clouds.

自由之鸟,
你的声音,
飞进我睡巢,
我困乏的翅膀
梦想飞向
云上之光。

244

I miss the meaning of my own part in the play of life
because I know not of the parts that others play.

> 我不懂人生大剧中
> 我角色的意义
> 因我对他人的角色
> 一无所知。

245

The flower sheds all its petals and finds the fruit.

> 花朵落尽花瓣
> 果实就会显现。

246

I leave my songs behind me to the bloom of the ever-returning honeysuckles and the joy of the wind from the south.

> 我在身后
> 留下我的歌
> 留给岁岁绽放的忍冬花，
> 留给南方吹来的欢乐的风。

247

Dead leaves when they lose themselves in soil take part in the life of the forest.

> 枯叶葬于土壤时
> 便与森林的生命
> 融为一体。

248

The mind ever seeks its words from its sounds and silence as the sky from its darkness and light.

> 心灵从其声音和宁静中寻辞
> 如天在黑暗和光间寻语。

249

The unseen dark plays on his flute and the rhythm of light eddies into stars and suns, into thoughts and dreams.

> 看不见的黑暗
> 吹着诗琴，
> 光的节奏
> 旋入太阳繁星
> 旋入思想与梦。

250

My songs are to sing that I have loved Thy singing.

> 我的歌唱到
> 我爱上你的歌唱。

251

When the voice of the Silent touches my words I know
him and therefore I know myself.

> 当沉默之音
> 触动我的言辞
> 我懂了他
> 因此懂了自己。

252

My last salutations are to them who knew me
imperfect and loved me.

我最后的致敬
献给知我不完美
仍爱我的人。

253

Love's gift cannot be given, it waits to be accepted.

爱之礼不给予，
它等待着被接受。

254

When death comes and whispers to me, "Thy days are ended," let me say to him, "I have lived in love and not in mere time."

He will ask, "Will thy songs remain?"

I shall say, "I know not, but this I know that often when I sang I found my eternity."

死神走近对我低语:

"你活到头了。"

让我对他说:

"我活在爱中,未虚度光阴。"

他会问:

"你的歌长存?"

我会说:

"我不知道,

但我知道我歌唱时

我找到了我的永恒。"

255

"Let me light my lamp," says the star, "and never debate if it will help to remove the darkness."

"让我点亮灯,"

星星说,

"不要争论我这盏灯

是否能消除黑暗。"

256

Before the end of my journey may I reach within myself the one which is the all, leaving the outer shell to float away with the drifting multitude upon the current of chance and change.

旅途结束前
愿我在我的灵魂里
抵达包容一切的我，
留下我的躯壳
随漂泊的众生
在机遇与变化的洪流中
一同漂去。

附:

采果之歌

Fruit-Gathering

（原著：[印]泰戈尔　黄建滨、黄尚戎译）

1

Bid me and I shall gather my fruits to bring them in full baskets into your courtyard, though some are lost and some not ripe.

For the season grows heavy with its fulness, and there is a plaintive shepherd's pipe in the shade.

Bid me and I shall set sail on the river.

The March wind is fretful, fretting the languid waves into murmurs.

The garden has yielded its all, and in the weary hour of evening the call comes from your house on the shore in the sunset.

你吩咐，我就采下果实装满筐送到你的庭院，尽管有的掉落有的未熟。

这一季丰收在望果实累累，树荫下传来牧童哀怨的笛声。

你吩咐，我就河上扬帆启程。

烦躁的三月风，吹得倦怠的波浪汩汩响。

果园结出全部果实，在令人疲乏的黄昏，从你岸边的房子传来夕阳中的呼唤。

2

My life when young was like a flower—a flower that loosens a petal or two from her abundance and never feels the loss when the spring breeze comes to beg at her door.

Now at the end of youth my life is like a fruit, having nothing to spare, and waiting to offer herself completely with her full burden of sweetness.

年轻时我生命如鲜花，当春风来到她门前乞讨，她从繁茂花瓣中取下一两瓣，却未感觉到有什么损失。

如今青春已逝，我的命如果实，已经无物施舍，正在等着把自己和满满的甜蜜完全奉献出来。

3

Is summer's festival only for fresh blossoms and not also for withered leaves and faded flowers?

Is the song of the sea in tune only with the rising waves?

Does it not also sing with the waves that fall?

Jewels are woven into the carpet where stands my king, but there are patient clods waiting to be touched by his feet.

Few are the wise and the great who sit by my Master, but he has taken the foolish in his arms and made me his servant for ever.

夏天的节日只为盛开的鲜花而不为枯叶和残花举办吗？

大海的歌是只和涨潮的波涛唱和吗？

它不是也在伴着落潮歌唱？

珠宝被织进我的国王踩着的地毯，耐心的泥土等待着国王双足接触。

我主旁边没坐几位智者和伟人，但是他把愚人拥抱怀中，而让我永远做他的仆人。

4

I woke and found his letter with the morning.

I do not know what it says, for I cannot read.

I shall leave the wise man alone with his books, I shall not trouble him, for who knows if he can read what the letter says.

Let me hold it to my forehead and press it to my heart.

When the night grows still and stars come out one by one I will spread it on my lap and stay silent.

The rustling leaves will read it aloud to me, the rushing stream will chant it, and the seven wise stars will sing it to me from the sky.

I cannot find what I seek, I cannot understand what I would learn; but this unread letter has lightened my burdens and turned my thoughts into songs.

醒来发现他的信与晨同到。

不知信里说什么，因我看不懂。

让智者独自去读他的书吧，我不会麻烦他，谁知他能否看懂信里的内容。

让我把信举到额前，贴到我的心口。

夜深人静繁星一颗颗闪现，我要把信摊在膝上静静坐着。

树叶沙沙作响为我朗读；溪水潺潺为我诵读；智慧七星将从天空为我唱读此信。

我找不到我所求，我也无法理解我将所知；未读之信减轻了我的负担，把我所想转化为歌。

5

A handful of dust could hide your signal when I did not know its meaning.

Now that I am wiser I read it in all that hid it before.

It is painted in petals of flowers; waves flash it from their foam; hills hold it high on their summits.

I had my face turned from you, therefore I read the letters awry and knew not their meaning.

当我不理解你信号之意，一掬土即把它掩盖。

既然我聪明多了，我透过屏障领悟其意。

它画在鲜花花瓣上；海浪泡沫使它闪烁；群山将它高擎峰巅。

我转过脸不看你，结果曲解了你的信，不明白其中含义。

6

Where roads are made I lose my way.

In the wide water, in the blue sky there is no line of a track.

The pathway is hidden by the birds' wings, by the star-fires, by the flowers of the wayfaring seasons.

And I ask my heart if its blood carries the wisdom of the unseen way.

铺路之处我迷了路。

无垠的海面，蔚蓝天空，都没有路的踪迹。

路被鸟的羽翼、灿烂星火、四季变化的花遮住。

我问我心，心血有否智慧找到那看不见的路？

7

Alas, I cannot stay in the house, and home has become no home to me, for the eternal Stranger calls, he is going along the road.

The sound of his footfall knocks at my breast; it pains me!

The wind is up, the sea is moaning.

I leave all my cares and doubts to follow the homeless tide, for the Stranger calls me, he is going along the road.

唉，我不能留在这屋里，这家已经不再是我家，永恒异乡人在呼唤，他正沿着道路走来。

他的足音敲击我胸膛，令我痛苦！

狂风骤起，大海在呜咽。

我抛开烦恼疑惑追逐无家海浪，因为异乡人在呼唤，他正沿着道路走来。

8

Be ready to launch forth, my heart! And let those linger who must.

For your name has been called in the morning sky.

Wait for none!

The desire of the bud is for the night and dew, but the blown flower cries for the freedom of light.

Burst your sheath, my heart, and come forth!

准备动身吧，我的心！让该留下的留下。

晨空中已传来对你的呼唤。

别等待！

蓓蕾所企盼的是暗夜和露珠，盛开的花朵渴求着光的自由。

冲破剑鞘，心，前进吧！

9

When I lingered among my hoarded treasure I felt like a worm that feeds in the dark upon the fruit where it was born.

I leave this prison of decay.

I care not to haunt the mouldy stillness, for I go in search of everlasting youth; I throw away all that is not one with my life nor as light as my laughter.

I run through time and, O my heart, in your chariot dances the poet who sings while he wanders.

徘徊于贮藏的珍宝，我觉得自己像蛀虫，在黑暗中吃着滋生它的果实。

我离开这腐朽牢狱。

我不愿出没腐朽静止中，因我要去寻找永久的青春；不似我笑声轻盈、无关我生命的一切，我都抛弃。

我穿越时间，噢，心啊，在你的战车里，吟游的诗人欢歌载舞。

10

You took my hand and drew me to your side, made me sit on the high seat before all men, till I became timid, unable to stir and walk my own way; doubting and debating at every step lest I should tread upon any thorn of their disfavour.

I am freed at last!

The blow has come, the drum of insult sounded, my seat is laid low in the dust.

My paths are open before me.

My wings are full of the desire of the sky.

I go to join the shooting stars of midnight, to plunge into the profound shadow.

I am like the storm-driven cloud of summer that, having cast off its crown of gold, hangs as a sword the thunderbolt upon a chain of lightning.

In desperate joy I run upon the dusty path of the despised; I draw near to your final welcome.

The child finds its mother when it leaves her womb.

When I am parted from you, thrown out from your household, I am free to see your face.

你牵我的手，把我拉到你身边，让我在众人面前坐在高处，直至我羞怯，不能动弹，也不能随意行走；每走一步我都满是矛盾犹疑，唯恐踩到众人冷漠的荆棘上。

终于自由了！
打击降临，凌辱之鼓敲响，我的座椅掉落尘土中。
我的路在面前展开。

我的翅膀充满冲天的渴望。
我要加入子夜的流星之中，纵身投入深邃的阴影。

像被暴风雨驱赶的夏日浮云，我抛下金色的王冠，把雷霆系于道道闪电，犹如佩上利剑。

绝望欢乐中我在被鄙视者的尘土路上奔跑，迎向你那最后的迎接。

婴儿离开子宫发现了母亲。

当我被赶出你家门，被迫离开你，便可自由看你的脸。

11

It decks me only to mock me, this jewelled chain of mine.

It bruises me when on my neck, it strangles me when I struggle to tear it off.

It grips my throat, it chokes my singing.

Could I but offer it to your hand, my Lord, I would be saved.

Take it from me, and in exchange bind me to you with a garland, for I am ashamed to stand before you with this jewelled chain on my neck.

装饰我只为嘲弄我，我这珠宝项链。

戴我颈上弄得我痛，我要扯下它，它却紧紧勒住我。

卡我喉咙，抑制我歌唱。

我的神，若能把它献你手上，我即得救。

把它拿走，换一束花环把我系在你身边，因为戴着它站在你的面前，我感到羞愧无比。

12

Far below flowed the Jumna, swift and clear, above frowned the jutting bank.

Hills dark with the woods and scarred with the torrents were gathered around.

Govinda, the great Sikh teacher, sat on the rock reading scriptures, when Raghunath, his disciple, proud of his wealth, came and bowed to him and said, "I have brought my poor present unworthy of your acceptance."

Thus saying he displayed before the teacher a pair of gold bangles wrought with costly stones.

The master took up one of them, twirling it round his finger, and the diamonds darted shafts of light.

Suddenly it slipped from his hand and rolled down the bank into the water.

"Alas," screamed Raghunath, and jumped into the stream.

The teacher set his eyes upon his book, and the water held and hid what it stole and went its way.

The daylight faded when Raghunath came back to the teacher tired and dripping.

He panted and said, "I can still get it back if you show me where it fell."

The teacher took up the remaining bangle and threw it into the water, said, "It is there."

下方清澈朱木拿奔流，上方突出河岸皱眉。

周围群山林木森森，激流直下道道伤痕。

锡克教师尊戈文达端坐岩石，读着经文，自傲富贵的弟子罗胡纳特走过来，施礼道："我为您带来一份薄礼，不成敬意，恳请笑纳。"

说罢，他拿出一对镶着昂贵宝石的金镯，放到大师面前。

大师拿起一只金镯，套到手指上转动，宝石放射出一道道光芒。

突然，手镯从他手中滑落，滚下堤岸，掉进水中。

"啊！"罗胡纳特尖叫着，跳入河中。

大师的眼睛注视着经卷，河水卷住藏起所窃之物，奔流而去。

暮色茫茫，罗胡纳特回到大师身边，浑身透湿无力。

他气喘吁吁："告诉我手镯落在哪，我去找回它。"

大师拿起剩下的那只手镯，挥手扔进水里，说道："它就在那里。"

注：Jumna，朱木拿，印度北部的一条河，发源于喜马拉雅山脉，最终流入恒河。Govinda，戈文达，锡克教师尊；Raghunath，罗胡纳特，是其弟子之一。Sikh，锡克教，印度的一个宗教。

13

To move is to meet you every moment,

Fellow-traveller!

It is to sing to the falling of your feet.

He whom your breath touches does not glide by the shelter of the bank.

He spreads a reckless sail to the wind and rides the turbulent water.

He who throws his doors open and steps onward receives your greeting.

He does not stay to count his gain or to mourn his loss; his heart beats the drum for his march, for that is to march with you every step,

Fellow-traveller!

前行是为了时刻与你相遇。

我的旅伴！

为了和着你落地脚步歌唱。

和你呼吸与共者不会借河岸庇护溜走。

不顾一切迎风扬帆，他在汹涌的水面前行。

敞开大门举步前行的人将受你的欢迎。

他不会停下计算所得，哀叹所失；他的心擂响前进鼓点，因为是与你步步同行，

我的旅伴！

14

My portion of the best in this world will come from your hands: such was your promise.

Therefore your light glistens in my tears.

I fear to be led by others lest I miss you waiting in some road corner to be my guide.

I walk my own wilful way till my very folly tempts you to my door.

For I have your promise that my portion of the best in this world will come from your hands.

世界上我最好的一份将出自你手，你这样承诺。

你的光在我泪花中闪烁。

我怕别人引路而错过你，因为你等在街角，打算为我引路。

我任性地前行，直到我的愚蠢引你到我门口。

因为你曾经承诺，世界上我最好的一份将出自你手。

15

Your speech is simple, my Master, but not theirs who talk of you.

I understand the voice of your stars and the silence of your trees.

I know that my heart would open like a flower; that my life has filled itself at a hidden fountain.

Your songs, like birds from the lonely land of snow, are winging to build their nests in my heart against the warmth of its April, and I am content to wait for the merry season.

神啊，你的话简洁，说你的人并非如此。

我明白你星星般的声音和你树木般的沉默。

我知道我的心会如鲜花绽放；我的生命已经从隐泉得到充实。

你的歌如同孤寂雪原的鸟，正盼着飞到我的心头筑巢以迎四月的温暖，而我满心在等待这欢乐的季节。

16

They knew the way and went to seek you along the narrow lane, but I wandered abroad into the night for I was ignorant.

I was not schooled enough to be afraid of you in the dark, therefore I came upon your doorstep unaware.

The wise rebuked me and bade me be gone, for I had not come by the lane.

I turned away in doubt, but you held me fast, and their scolding became louder every day.

他们熟悉路，沿着狭窄小巷去找你，但我因为愚昧无知在茫茫黑夜里徘徊。

我受教育不够，在黑暗中并不害怕你，所以我不知不觉来到你门前。

聪明人训斥我命我离开，因为我没从小巷来。

我困惑地转身，但你紧拉我，于是他们的责骂日渐声大。

17

I brought out my earthen lamp from my house and cried, "Come, children, I will light your path!"

The night was still dark when I returned, leaving the road to its silence, crying, "Light me, O Fire! for my earthen lamp lies broken in the dust!"

我从家里拿出陶灯，叫道："孩子们，来，我给你们照路！"

归来时天色依旧漆黑，不管道路的寂静，我高喊："火啊，为我照明！我的陶灯破在了尘土里！"

18

No: it is not yours to open buds into blossoms.

Shake the bud, strike it; it is beyond your power to make it blossom.

Your touch soils it, you tear its petals to pieces and strew them in the dust.

But no colours appear, and no perfume.

Ah! It is not for you to open the bud into a blossom.

He who can open the bud does it so simply.

He gives it a glance, and the life-sap stirs through its veins.

At his breath the flower spreads its wings and flutters in the wind.

Colours flush out like heart-longings, the perfume betrays a sweet secret.

He who can open the bud does it so simply.

不，不是你的力量让蓓蕾开的花。

你摇它，打它；你的力量无法让蓓蕾开花。

你的触摸弄脏了它，你撕碎花瓣，撒在尘土中。

没有绚丽色彩，没有芬芳。

哎呀！并不是要用你的力量让蓓蕾开花。

能够让蓓蕾开花，其实很简单。

他瞥上一眼，生命之液颤动叶脉。

吹一口气，花朵便展开翅膀随风起舞。

色彩喷涌如心灵热望，芬芳泄露甜美秘密。

能够让蓓蕾开花，其实很简单。

19

Sudâs, the gardener, plucked from his tank the last lotus left by the ravage of winter and went to sell it to the king at the palace gate.

There he met a traveller who said to him, "Ask your price for the last lotus, —I shall offer it to Lord Buddha."

Sudâs said, "If you pay one golden mâshâ it will be yours."

The traveller paid it.

At that moment the king came out and he wished to buy the flower, for he was on his way to see Lord Buddha, and he thought, "It would be a fine thing to lay at his feet the lotus that bloomed in winter."

When the gardener said he had been offered a golden mâshâ the king offered him ten, but the traveller doubled the price.

The gardener, being greedy, imagined a greater gain from him for whose sake they were bidding. He bowed and said, "I cannot sell this lotus."

In the hushed shade of the mango grove beyond the city wall Sudâs stood before Lord Buddha, on whose lips sat the silence of love and whose eyes beamed peace like the morning star of the dew-washed autumn.

Sudâs looked in his face and put the lotus at his feet and bowed his head to the dust.

Buddha smiled and asked, "What is your wish, my son?"

Sudâs cried, "The least touch of your feet."

花匠苏达斯从他池塘里摘下严冬留下的最后一朵莲花，来到皇宫门前，向国王出售。

在那里他遇到一个旅人，旅人问他："最后的这朵莲花多少钱？我想献给佛陀。"

苏达斯说："你付一枚金币，我就卖给你。"

旅人付了钱。

这时国王走了出来，也很希望买下这朵莲花，因为他要去朝拜佛陀，他心想："把这冬天开放的莲花献于佛陀脚下，再好不过。"

花匠说他已经收下一枚金币，国王说他愿出十枚，但旅人愿出双倍的钱。

贪心花匠见他们为佛陀抬价，就想到佛陀那里赚更多钱。他鞠躬说道："这花我不卖了。"

在城外杧果林寂静的树荫下，苏达斯站到了佛陀的面前。佛陀唇边布满无声的爱，目光宁静，如露水洗过的秋日的晨星。

苏达斯看着他的脸，莲花放到他脚边，俯首叩拜于地。

佛陀笑道："孩子，你想要什么？"

他高叫："就碰碰你的脚。"

注：mâshâ 为印度货币单位。

20

Make me thy poet, O Night, veiled Night!

There are some who have sat speechless for ages in thy shadow; let me utter their songs.

Take me up on thy chariot without wheels, running noiselessly from world to world, thou queen in the palace of time, thou darkly beautiful!

Many a questioning mind has stealthily entered thy courtyard and roamed through thy lampless house seeking for answers.

From many a heart, pierced with the arrow of joy from the hands of the Unknown, have burst forth glad chants, shaking the darkness to its foundation.

Those wakeful souls gaze in the starlight in wonder at the treasure they have suddenly found.

Make me their poet, O Night, the poet of thy fathomless silence.

夜，我做你诗人，面纱夜！

有些人在你阴影中默默坐了很久，让我唱他们的歌。

把我带上你的无轮战车，无声穿越一个又一个世界，你是时间宫殿皇的后，黝黑美人！

　　许多探究的心灵偷偷进入你的庭院，在你无灯的屋中徘徊，寻求答案。

　　从许多被未知者手中欢乐之箭射穿的心里，爆发出明快的颂歌，震撼了黑暗的根基。

　　灵魂警醒诧异地凝视星光，看着他们突然发现的宝藏。

　　让我做他们的诗人，啊，黑夜，吟你深邃寂静。

21

I will meet one day the Life within me, the joy that hides in my life, though the days perplex my path with their idle dust.

I have known it in glimpses, and its fitful breath has come upon me, making my thoughts fragrant for a while.

I will meet one day the Joy without me that dwells behind the screen of light—and will stand in the overflowing solitude where all things are seen as by their creator.

　　我终会在自己身上遇见生命，命中隐藏的欢乐，尽管岁月用闲尘困住我的路。

　　我已多次瞥见它，它的气息阵阵袭来，使我的思绪一时充满馨香。

终有一天我会在身外遇见光明幕后的欢乐——我站在充溢的孤独中，那里，万事万物尽在造物主眼中。

22

This autumn morning is tired with excess of light, and if your songs grow fitful and languid give me your flute awhile.

I shall but play with it as the whim takes me, —now take it on my lap, now touch it with my lips, now keep it by my side on the grass.

But in the solemn evening stillness I shall gather flowers, to deck it with wreaths, I shall fill it with fragrance; I shall worship it with the lighted lamp.

Then at night I shall come to you and give you back your flute.

You will play on it the music of midnight when the lonely crescent moon wanders among the stars.

光照强烈，秋天的清晨感到疲倦，把长笛给我，既然你的歌慵懒，断断续续。

我要随心所欲地吹奏长笛，——时而放在膝上，时而放在唇边，时而放在身边草地上。

但是在庄严肃穆的夜晚我采集鲜花，用花环装饰长笛，让它充满馨香，点亮灯火来把它供奉。

入夜，我会回到你身边，把长笛还你。

当一轮寂寞的新月在繁星间游荡，你将会吹奏起午夜乐章。

23

The poet's mind floats and dances on the waves of life amidst the voices of wind and water.

Now when the sun has set and the darkened sky draws upon the sea like drooping lashes upon a weary eye it is time to take away his pen, and let his thoughts sink into the bottom of the deep amid the eternal secret of that silence.

在风声和水声之间诗人的思绪在生命之波上飘荡起舞。

现在太阳已落山，暗黑天空如下垂的睫毛挂在倦怠的眼上贴近海面，是该拿走他的笔了；让他的思想沉入深渊之底，去到那宁静而永恒的秘密之中。

24

The night is dark and your slumber is deep in the hush of my being.

Wake, O Pain of Love, for I know not how to open the door, and I stand outside.

The hours wait, the stars watch, the wind is still, the silence is heavy in my heart.

Wake, Love, wake! Brim my empty cup, and with a breath of song ruffle the night.

漆黑之夜，你深睡在我静寂的存在之中。
醒来，爱情之苦，我不知道怎样开门，只好站在门外。

时间在等，繁星在看，风已平息，我心中寂静沉沉。
醒醒吧，爱情！灌满空杯，用歌的气息撩动静夜。

25

The bird of the morning sings.

Whence has he word of the morning before the morning breaks, and when the dragon night still holds the sky in its cold black coils?

Tell me, bird of the morning, how, through the twofold night of the sky and the leaves, he found his way into your dream, the messenger out of the east?

The world did not believe you when you cried, "The sun is on his way, the night is no more."

O sleeper, awake!

Bare your forehead, waiting for the first blessing of light, and sing with the bird of the morning in glad faith.

清晨的鸟在歌唱。

黎明未现，暗夜之龙仍用冰冷黑色盘绕天空，晨鸟能在哪里找到清晨的歌词？

清晨的鸟，告诉我，东方使者怎样通过天空树叶的双重黑夜，找到了通往你梦中的道路？

当你高叫"太阳上路，黑夜将逝"之时，世界并不相信你。

啊，睡者，醒来！

露出额头，等待第一缕阳光的祝福，怀着喜悦虔诚，和晨鸟同欢唱。

26

The beggar in me lifted his lean hands to the starless sky and cried into night's ear with his hungry voice.

His prayers were to the blind Darkness who lay like a fallen god in a desolate heaven of lost hopes.

The cry of desire eddied round a chasm of despair, a wailing bird circling its empty nest.

But when morning dropped anchor at the rim of the East, the beggar in me leapt and cried:

"Blessed am I that the deaf night denied me—that its coffer was empty."

He cried, "O Life, O Light, you are precious! and precious is the joy that at last has known you!"

我内心的乞丐向无星天空举起瘦手，用饥饿之声对夜的耳朵呼喊。

他向躺在无望孤寂天国的如落下神坛的神祇的盲眼黑暗祈求。

祈求的叫喊在失望的深渊回旋，哀鸣的鸟在空巢上盘旋。

当清晨在东方的边缘抛锚，我内心的乞丐跳起大叫：

"幸亏耳聋的夜拒绝了我——它早已囊空如洗。"

他道："啊，生命，啊，光明，你们珍贵！与你们相识之
乐也珍贵！"

27

Sanâtan was telling his beads by the Ganges when a
Brahmin in rags came to him and said, "Help me, I am poor!"

"My alms-bowl is all that is my own," said Sanâtan, "I have
given away everything I had."

"But my Lord Shiva came to me in my dreams," said the
Brahmin, "and counselled me to come to you."

Sanâtan suddenly remembered he had picked up a stone
without price among the pebbles on the river-bank, and thinking
that some one might need it hid it in the sands.

He pointed out the spot to the Brahmin, who's wondering
dug up the stone.

The Brahmin sat on the earth and mused alone till the sun
went down behind the trees, and cowherds went home with their
cattle.

Then he rose and came slowly to Sanâtan and said, "Master,
give me the least fraction of the wealth that disdains all the

wealth of the world."

And he threw the precious stone into the water.

恒河边，沙那坦数着念珠，一个衣衫褴褛的婆罗门走来说："帮我，我很穷！"

"我的乞碗是我的全部。"沙那坦说，"我已施舍完我所有的一切。"

"但是我主湿婆托梦给我，"婆罗门说，"他建议我找你帮忙。"

沙那坦突然想起他在河边的鹅卵石中捡到过一块无价的宝石，心想，也许会有人需要，就把它埋在沙中。

他把藏宝点指给婆罗门，他惊异地挖出宝石。

婆罗门坐在地上独自沉思，直到太阳从树后落下，牧人赶着牛群回了家。

他起身慢慢走到沙那坦跟前说："大师，有种财富蔑视一切财富，赐我哪怕一点也行。"

说罢，他把珍贵宝石扔进河里。

注：Sanâtan，沙那坦，印度教导师。the Ganges，恒河。Brahmin，婆罗门，印度最高的种姓。Shiva，湿婆，印度教三大主神之一。

28

Time after time I came to your gate with raised hands, asking for more and yet more.

You gave and gave, now in slow measure, now in sudden excess.

I took some, and some things I let drop; some lay heavy on my hands; some I made into playthings and broke them when tired; till the wrecks and the hoard of your gifts grew immense, hiding you, and the ceaseless expectation wore my heart out.

Take, oh take—has now become my cry.

Shatter all from this beggar's bowl: put out this lamp of the importunate watcher; hold my hands, raise me from the still-gathering heap of your gifts into the bare infinity of your uncrowded presence.

我一次次来到你的门边，举手，求你赏赐再赏赐。

你给了又给，有时很少，有时突然很多。

我接过一些，掉落一些；有些沉沉在手上；有些变成玩具，玩腻了就打坏；直到破的、收藏的礼物堆积并遮住你，无休止的期望耗尽我的心灵。

拿去，拿去吧——我呼喊着。

砸碎乞丐碗里的一切：熄灭讨厌的观察者的灯火；拉着我的手，把我拖出你仍在聚积的礼物堆，去到你独自存在的赤裸无限中。

29

You have set me among those who are defeated.

I know it is not for me to win, nor to leave the game.

I shall plunge into the pool although but to sink to the bottom.

I shall play the game of my undoing.

I shall stake all I have and when I lose my last penny I shall stake myself, and then I think I shall have won through my utter defeat.

你已把我置于失败者的行列。

我知道我赢不了，也不肯离开比赛。

我将纵身跳入池中，即使可能沉到池底。

我要参加这必败之赛。

我将押上我的全部，最后输光，再把自己作赌注，这时我想，我将会通过完败而获胜。

30

A smile of mirth spread over the sky when you dressed my heart in rags and sent her forth into the road to beg.

She went from door to door, and many a time when her bowl was nearly full she was robbed.

At the end of the weary day she came to your palace gate holding up her pitiful bowl, and you came and took her hand and seated her beside you on your throne.

天空绽放欢愉微笑，当你给我的心穿上褴褛衣裳，让她沿街乞讨。

她挨家乞讨，好几次她的碗要盛满，她又被抢劫一空。

疲惫的一天将尽，她手捧可怜的乞碗来到你宫殿门前，你上前牵起她的手，让她到宝座坐在你身边。

31

"Who among you will take up the duty of feeding the hungry?" Lord Buddha asked his followers when famine raged at Shravasti.

Ratnâkar, the banker, hung his head and said, "Much more is needed than all my wealth to feed the hungry."

Jaysen, the chief of the King's army, said, "I would gladly give my life's blood, but there is not enough food in my house."

Dharmapâl, who owned broad acres of land, said with a sigh, "The drought demon has sucked my fields dry. I know not how to pay King's dues."

Then rose Supriyâ, the mendicant's daughter.
She bowed to all and meekly said, "I will feed the hungry."
"How!" they cried in surprise. "How can you hope to fulfil that vow?"

"I am the poorest of you all," said Supriyâ, "that is my strength. I have my coffer and my store at each of your houses."

"你们当中谁愿意承担救济灾民的重任？"斯拉瓦西斯蒂城闹饥荒时，佛陀问门徒。

银行家罗特纳卡低下头说："我的财富远远不够救济灾民。"

国王军队首领查亚森说："为灾民我愿献出生命之血，但我家食物不够。"

　　田产巨大的达姆帕尔叹道："干旱恶魔吸干了我的土地。我不知怎样向国王缴税。"

　　乞丐女儿苏波莉雅站出来。

　　她鞠躬施礼，温顺地说道："我愿救灾。"

　　"什么？"众人惊呼，"你靠什么履行诺言？"

　　"你们中我最穷，"苏波莉雅说，"我就靠这。在座诸位家中都有我的钱柜、粮仓。"

　　注：Shravasti，斯拉瓦西斯蒂，又译舍卫，古印度城市。

32

My king was unknown to me, therefore when he claimed his tribute I was bold to think I would hide myself leaving my debts unpaid.

I fled and fled behind my day's work and my night's dreams.

But his claims followed me at every breath I drew.

Thus I came to know that I am known to him and no place left which is mine.

Now I wish to lay my all before his feet, and gain the right to my place in his kingdom.

我并不认识国王，所以当他要求进贡时，我冒失地想，我可以躲起来，不去还债。

白天工作，夜晚做梦，我逃了又逃。
但他的讨债紧跟我次次呼吸。
于是我明白国王认识我，这世上我无处可躲。

现在我要把一切献给他，获取在他王国的立足权利。

33

When I thought I would mould you, an image from my life for men to worship, I brought my dust and desires and all my coloured delusions and dreams.

When I asked you to mould with my life an image from your heart for you to love, you brought your fire and force, and truth, loveliness and peace.

我想以我的生命来塑造你的形象供人膜拜，我拿来我的尘土、欲望、五彩的幻觉和梦想。

我请求你依你的心塑造我的生命形象让你爱，你拿来你的火、力、真理、爱与宁静。

34

"Sire," announced the servant to the King, "the saint Narottam has never deigned to enter your royal temple.

"He is singing God's praise under the trees by the open road. The temple is empty of worshippers.

"They flock round him like bees round the white lotus, leaving the golden jar of honey unheeded."

The King, vexed at heart, went to the spot where Narottam sat on the grass.

He asked him, "Father, why leave my temple of the golden dome and sit on the dust outside to preach God's love?"

"Because God is not there in your temple," said Narottam.

The King frowned and said, "Do you know, twenty millions of gold went to the making of that marvel of art, and it was consecrated to God with costly rites?"

"Yes, I know it," answered Narottam. "It was in that year when thousands of your people whose houses had been burned stood vainly asking for help at your door.

"And God said, 'The poor creature who can give no shelter to his brothers would build my house!'

"And he took his place with the shelterless under the trees by the road.

"And that golden bubble is empty of all but hot vapour of pride."

The King cried in anger, "Leave my land."

Calmly said the saint, "Yes, banish me where you have banished my God."

"陛下，"仆人通报国王，"圣者纳罗达姆从不肯屈尊到您的皇家神庙。"

"他在大路边的树下吟唱颂圣之歌。神庙里已没人来做朝拜。"

"他们聚在他身边，像蜜蜂围着白莲，而不理睬金色的蜜坛。"

国王很恼火，去找坐在草地上的纳罗达姆。

他问："师父，你为何离开金顶神庙，坐在门外尘土中赞颂天帝的爱？"

"因为天帝不在神庙。"纳罗达姆答道。

国王皱眉说："你知道，我花了两千万两金子建造那艺术奇迹，举行豪华仪式把它奉献给了天帝。"

"是，我知道。"纳罗达姆答道，"正是那一年，您成千上万的子民房屋被烧，到您宫门前求助却枉然。

"天帝说：'可怜的国王不给同胞避难之处，却为我建庙！'

"所以他到路边树下与无家可归的人一起。

"那个黄金气泡除了高傲的热气一无所有。"

国王怒吼："快滚出我国！"

圣者平静地说："好，赶我到您放逐天帝之地。"

35

The trumpet lies in the dust.

The wind is weary, the light is dead.

Ah, the evil day!

Come, fighters, carrying your flags, and singers, with your war-songs!

Come, pilgrims of the march, hurrying on your journey!

The trumpet lies in the dust waiting for us.

I was on my way to the temple with my evening offerings, seeking for a place of rest after the day's dusty toil: hoping my hurts would be healed and the stains in my garment washed white, when I found thy trumpet lying in the dust.

Was it not the hour for me to light my evening lamp?

Had not the night sung its lullaby to the stars?

O thou blood-red rose, my poppies of sleep have paled and faded!

I was certain my wanderings were over and my debts all paid when suddenly I came upon thy trumpet lying in the dust.

Strike my drowsy heart with thy spell of youth!

Let my joy in life blaze up in fire.

Let the shafts of awakening fly through the heart of night, and a thrill of dread shake blindness and palsy.

I have come to raise thy trumpet from the dust.

Sleep is no more for me—my walk shall be through showers of arrows.

Some shall run out of their houses and come to my side—some shall weep.

Some in their beds shall toss and groan in dire dreams.

For to-night thy trumpet shall be sounded.

From thee I have asked peace only to find shame.

Now I stand before thee—help me to put on my armour!

Let hard blows of trouble strike fire into my life.

Let my heart beat in pain, the drum of thy victory.

My hands shall be utterly emptied to take up thy trumpet.

号角躺在尘埃里。

风已疲倦了，光已熄灭。

啊，不幸之日！

来，战士们，高举军旗，歌手们，唱起战歌！

来，朝圣者们，踏上征程快步前进！

尘埃里号角在等着我们。

我带着晚祷祭品赶往神庙，经过一天尘土折磨去寻找休息之地；希望创伤能治愈，衣服的污渍能洗干净，这时，我发现你的号角躺在尘埃里。

是不是该我点亮夜灯的时刻到了？

黑夜还没给星星唱摇篮曲吗？

啊，血红玫瑰，我睡眠之花已褪色凋零！

我敢肯定我的漂泊已结束，我的债务已还清，突然，我发现你的号角躺在尘埃里。

用青春魔咒敲我的懒心！

让生命欢乐在火中燃烧。

让正醒来的利箭刺透黑夜之心，让一阵恐怖震撼盲从和麻木。

我已从尘埃中捡起了号角。

不再沉睡——我将徒步穿过阵雨般的利箭。

有人跑出房屋来到我的身边，有人哭泣。

有人床上辗转，在噩梦中呻吟。

因为今晚你的号角将吹响。

我向你祈求和平，却只得来羞愧。

现在我站在你面前——帮我穿上盔甲！

让沉重打击把火注进我生命。

让我的心痛敲响胜利的战鼓。

我将腾出我的双手去接过你的号角。

36

When, mad in their mirth, they raised dust to soil thy robe, O Beautiful, it made my heart sick.

I cried to thee and said, "Take thy rod of punishment and judge them."

The morning light struck upon those eyes, red with the revel of night; the place of the white lily greeted their burning breath; the stars through the depth of the sacred dark stared at their carousing—at those that raised dust to soil thy robe, O Beautiful!

Thy judgment seat was in the flower garden, in the birds' notes in springtime: in the shady river-banks, where the trees muttered in answer to the muttering of the waves.

O my Lover, they were pitiless in their passion.

They prowled in the dark to snatch thy ornaments to deck their own desires.

When they had struck thee and thou wert pained, it pierced me to the quick, and I cried to thee and said, "Take thy sword, O my Lover, and judge them!"

Ah, but thy justice was vigilant.

A mother's tears were shed on their insolence; the imperishable faith of a lover hid their spears of rebellion in its own wounds.

Thy judgment was in the mute pain of sleepless love: in the blush of the chaste: in the tears of the night of the desolate: in the pale morning-light of forgiveness.

O Terrible, they in their reckless greed climbed thy gate at night, breaking into thy storehouse to rob thee.

But the weight of their plunder grew immense, too heavy to carry or to remove.

Thereupon I cried to thee and said, Forgive them, O Terrible!

Thy forgiveness burst in storms, throwing them down, scattering their thefts in the dust.

Thy forgiveness was in the thunder-stone; in the shower of blood; in the angry red of the sunset.

噢，美人，当他们狂喜扬尘弄脏你衣裙，我很痛心。

我向你高喊道："拿起惩罚之棒审判他们。"

晨光照着夜晚狂欢熬红的眼睛，长满白百合之地迎着他们燃烧的气息；星星透过神圣黑暗瞪着他们痛饮，瞪着扬尘弄脏你衣裙的人，噢，美人！

你把审判席设在花园，设在春鸟的歌声里：设在绿树成荫的岸边，那里树木悄声细语回应波浪的低语。

噢，我的爱人，他们纵情绝无怜惜。

他们在暗中潜行，攫取你的饰物满足私欲。

当他们打你，令你痛苦时，他们也刺痛了我，我喊道："快出剑，噢，我的爱人，审判他们。"

啊，你的正义始终警醒。

你为他们的无礼流下母亲的泪；爱人不朽的忠贞把他们反叛的剑藏进自己伤口。

你的审判是不眠之爱的无言之苦、贞女脸上的红晕、孤寂者的夜之眼泪、宽厚之心那苍白的晨曦。

噢，可惧之神，他们贪婪无比，深夜爬进你的家门，闯进库房抢劫。

但他们的赃物越来越重，使得他们扛不走搬不动。

于是我对你高喊："宽恕他们，噢，可惧之神！"

你的宽恕在雷雨中爆发，击倒他们，赃物撒在土中。

你的宽恕融于陨落雷石，融于阵阵血雨，融于愤怒的夕阳红中。

37

Upagupta, the disciple of Buddha, lay asleep on the dust by the city wall of Mathura.

Lamps were all out, doors were all shut, and stars were all hidden by the murky sky of August.

Whose feet were those tinkling with anklets, touching his breast of a sudden?

He woke up startled, and the light from a woman's lamp struck his forgiving eyes.

It was the dancing girl, starred with jewels, clouded with a pale-blue mantle, drunk with the wine of her youth.

She lowered her lamp and saw the young face, austerely beautiful.

"Forgive me, young ascetic," said the woman; "graciously come to my house. The dusty earth is not a fit bed for you."

The ascetic answered, "Woman, go on your way; when the time is ripe I will come to you."

Suddenly the black night showed its teeth in a flash of lightning.

The storm growled from the corner of the sky, and the woman trembled in fear.

. . .

The branches of the wayside trees were aching with blossom.

Gay notes of the flute came floating in the warm spring air from afar.

The citizens had gone to the woods, to the festival of flowers.

From the mid-sky gazed the full moon on the shadows of the silent town.

The young ascetic was walking in the lonely street, while overhead the lovesick koels urged from the mango branches their sleepless plaint.

Upagupta passed through the city gates, and stood at the base of the rampart.

What woman lay in the shadow of the wall at his feet, struck with the black pestilence, her body spotted with sores, hurriedly driven away from the town?

The ascetic sat by her side, taking her head on his knees, and moistened her lips with water and smeared her body with balm.

"Who are you, merciful one?" asked the woman.

"The time, at last, has come to visit you, and I am here," replied the young ascetic.

佛陀弟子乌波库勃多躺在穆图拉城墙边的尘土上酣然入睡。

灯火熄灭,门户关闭,星星们都躲进了八月黑暗的天空。

是谁的脚镯叮当作响,突然触到他的胸膛?

他突然惊醒,女人手中的灯光照着他慈悲的眼睛。

来者是个舞女,珠光宝气,披着淡蓝色的斗篷,陶醉于青春美酒。

她放低灯,看到他稳重俊美的年轻脸庞。

"请原谅,年轻的苦行僧,"她说,"请赏光到我家吧。尘土地不是你合适的卧床。"

　　苦行僧答道:"女人啊,你走吧;时机成熟我会去找你的。"
突然, 黑夜用一束闪电露出它的牙齿。
暴风雨从天边呼啸而来, 女人吓得瑟瑟发抖。

······

　　路边的树枝经历着开花时的阵痛。
春天温暖的空气中, 远方飘来欢快笛声。
城里的男女老少来到树林参加百花佳节。
一轮圆月从半空注视着寂静城市的阴影。

　　年轻的苦行僧走在孤寂的街道, 头上, 相思的杜鹃们在
杧果枝中倾诉不眠的哀怨。
　　乌波库勃多经过一道道城门, 站到了护城墙下。
　　在城墙阴影之中躺着一个患鼠疫的女人, 她全身溃烂,
被人匆匆赶出城外。这个女人到底是谁?

　　苦行僧坐在她身边, 把她的头放在膝上, 用水润她嘴唇,
用香膏敷她全身。
　　"慈悲的人, 你是谁? "女人问道。
　　"看望你的时刻来临,于是我就来了。"年轻的苦行僧道。

　　注: Upagupta, 又译优婆鞠多, 印度阿育王时代的佛教
大师。Mathura, 又译摩突罗, 古代中印度的一个国家。

38

This is no mere dallying of love between us, my lover.

Again and again have swooped down upon me the screaming nights of storm, blowing out my lamp: dark doubts have gathered, blotting out all stars from my sky.

Again and again the banks have burst, letting the flood sweep away my harvest, and wailing and despair have rent my sky from end to end.

This have I learnt that there are blows of pain in your love, never the cold apathy of death.

这只是我们之间的爱情游戏，爱人啊。

一次又一次，呼啸的暴风雨之夜向我猛扑过来，吹灭我的灯；黑暗疑云聚集，遮住我天空的星。

一次又一次，河堤坍塌，洪水把我的庄稼冲走，悲痛和绝望把我整个天空彻底撕碎。

我明白了，你的爱情里有痛苦打击，绝无死亡的无情冷漠。

39

The wall breaks asunder, light, like divine laughter, bursts in.

Victory, O Light!

The heart of the night is pierced!

With your flashing sword cut in twain the tangle of doubt and feeble desires!

Victory!

Come, Implacable!

Come, you who are terrible in your whiteness.

O Light, your drum sounds in the march of fire, and the red torch is held on high; death dies in a burst of splendour!

墙壁坍塌，光明闯入，如神圣的笑声。

胜利，啊，光明！

黑夜心脏被撕碎！

用亮剑把纠结的怀疑、虚弱的欲望劈成两段。

胜利！

来，绝不宽容！

来，一片洁白的你如此可怖。

啊，光明，鼓声在火队中敲响，红色火炬高高举起；辉煌迸发，死亡必亡！

40

O fire, my brother, I sing victory to you.

You are the bright red image of fearful freedom.

You swing your arms in the sky, you sweep your impetuous fingers across the harp-string, your dance music is beautiful.

When my days are ended and the gates are opened you will burn to ashes this cordage of hands and feet.

My body will be one with you, my heart will be caught in the whirls of your frenzy, and the burning heat that was my life will flash up and mingle itself in your flame.

噢，火焰，兄弟，我为你歌唱胜利。

你是极端的自由的红色意象。

你在空中挥动着双臂，你的手指疯狂地掠过琴弦，你的舞曲美妙无比。

当我生命将尽，大门敞开，你将把绑住我手脚的绳索烧成灰烬。

我的身躯将融于你，我的心将卷进你狂热的旋转，我的生命是燃烧的热能，闪闪发光，融入你的火焰。

41

The Boatman is out crossing the wild sea at night.

The mast is aching because of its full sails filled with the violent wind.

Stung with the night's fang the sky falls upon the sea, poisoned with black fear.

The waves dash their heads against the dark unseen, and the Boatman is out crossing the wild sea.

The Boatman is out, I know not for what tryst, startling the night with the sudden white of his sails.

I know not at what shore, at last, he lands to reach the silent courtyard where the lamp is burning and to find her who sits in the dust and waits.

What is the quest that makes his boat care not for storm nor darkness?

Is it heavy with gems and pearls?

Ah, no, the Boatman brings with him no treasure, but only a white rose in his hand and a song on his lips.

It is for her who watches alone at night with her lamp burning.

She dwells in the wayside hut. Her loose hair flies in the wind and hides her eyes.

The storm shrieks through her broken doors, the light flickers in her earthen lamp flinging shadows on the walls.

Through the howl of the winds she hears him call her name, she whose name is unknown.

It is long since the Boatman sailed. It will be long before the day breaks and he knocks at the door.

The drums will not be beaten and none will know.

Only light shall fill the house, blessed shall be the dust, and the heart glad.

All doubts shall vanish in silence when the Boatman comes to the shore.

夜晚船夫起航，横渡汹涌大海。
因为船帆鼓满了狂风，桅杆感到痛苦不堪。
天空被夜之牙咬伤，中了恐怖黑毒，跌落海面。
浪峰朝着看不见的黑暗猛冲，船夫起航，横渡汹涌大海。

船夫已起航，我不知他将赴何约，用突现的白帆使黑夜震惊。

我不知他最终靠岸何处，他走向亮灯的寂静院落，寻找坐在尘土中等待着的她。

不畏风暴和黑暗，他的船要寻找什么？
它满载宝石和珍珠？

啊，不，船夫没有带任何珠宝，只有手里的一朵白玫瑰，双唇上的一支歌。
这是给她的，她在夜里亮着灯独自守候。

她住在路边小屋。
她的散发飘舞，挡住她双眼。
暴风雨呼啸，穿过她的破门,闪烁的陶灯把阴影投向四壁。
狂风怒吼，她听到他在叫她，她无人知晓之名。
船夫起航，已经很久。
还要很久很久天才会亮，他才会敲门。
没人敲鼓，没人知道他会来。
只有光照满屋，尘土得到祝福，心会愉悦。
船夫靠岸，一切疑问都会在静寂中消失。

42

I cling to this living raft, my body, in the narrow stream of my earthly years.

I leave it when the crossing is over.

And then?

I do not know if the light there and the darkness are the same.

The Unknown is the perpetual freedom:

He is pitiless in his love.

He crushes the shell for the pearl, dumb in the prison of the dark.

You muse and weep for the days that are done, poor heart!

Be glad that days are to come!

The hour strikes, O pilgrim!

It is time for you to take the parting of the ways!

His face will be unveiled once again and you shall meet.

紧附这活木筏，我的躯体，我漂在尘世岁月的窄溪。

渡过之后我便将它抛弃。

然后？

我不知那里的光明和黑暗是否一样。

未知者是那永恒的自由：

他的爱没有怜悯。

他打碎贝壳，寻找囚禁在暗中无言的珍珠。

可怜，心沉思，为逝去时日哭泣！

为将来日子欢欣！

朝圣者，钟已敲响！

你该做抉择的时刻已经来临！

他将再次揭开面纱，你们会相见。

43

Over the relic of Lord Buddha King Bimbisâr built a shrine, a salutation in white marble.

There in the evening would come all the brides and daughters of the King's house to offer flowers and light lamps.

When the son became king in his time he washed his father's creed away with blood, and lit sacrificial fires with its sacred books.

The autumn day was dying.

The evening hour of worship was near.

Shrimati, the queen's maid, devoted to Lord Buddha, having bathed in holy water, and decked the golden tray with lamps and fresh white blossoms, silently raised her dark eyes to the queen's face.

The queen shuddered in fear and said, "Do you not know, foolish girl, that death is the penalty for whoever brings worship to Buddha's shrine?

"Such is the king's will."

Shrimati bowed to the queen, and turning away from her door came and stood before Amitâ, the newly wed bride of the king's son.

A mirror of burnished gold on her lap, the newly wed bride was braiding her dark long tresses and painting the red spot of good luck at the parting of her hair.

Her hands trembled when she saw the young maid, and she cried, "What fearful peril would you bring me! Leave me this instant."

Princess Shuklâ sat at the window reading her book of romance by the light of the setting sun.

She started when she saw at her door the maid with the sacred offerings.

Her book fell down from her lap, and she whispered in Shrimati's ears, "Rush not to death, daring woman!"

Shrimati walked from door to door.

She raised her head and cried, "O women of the king's house, hasten!

"The time for our Lord's worship is come!"

Some shut their doors in her face and some reviled her.

The last gleam of daylight faded from the bronze dome of the palace tower.

Deep shadows settled in street corners: the bustle of the city was hushed: the gong at the temple of Shiva announced the time of the evening prayer.

In the dark of the autumn evening, deep as a limpid lake, stars throbbed with light, when the guards of the palace garden were startled to see through the trees a row of lamps burning at the shrine of Buddha.

They ran with their swords unsheathed, crying, "Who are you, foolish one, reckless of death?"

"I am Shrimati," replied a sweet voice, "the servant of Lord Buddha."

The next moment her heart's blood coloured the cold marble with its red.

And in the still hour of stars died the light of the last lamp of worship at the foot of the shrine.

国王宾婆沙罗用洁白大理石为佛陀圣骨建造神龛，以表敬意。

傍晚，王室所有的嫔妃公主都会来到这里，敬献鲜花，点燃明灯。

后来王子登基当上了国王，他用血洗去了父王的信条，用圣书点燃了献祭之火。

秋日将要逝去了。

做晚祷的时辰已经临近。

王后侍女斯丽马蒂虔信佛陀，她用圣水沐浴，用明灯和洁白鲜花装点好金盘，默默抬起乌黑双眼望着王后的脸。

王后惊恐万分，说道："傻姑娘，你不知道，凡是到佛陀神龛献祭的人都要被处以死刑？

"这是国王的旨意。"

斯丽马蒂向王后鞠躬施礼后，转身出门，来到了国王儿子的新娘阿米达的面前。

金灿灿的镜子搁在膝头，新娘正在把她乌黑的长发编成辫子，在额头的发际点一颗吉祥的红痣。

看到年轻侍女，她双手颤抖道："你想给我带来什么可怕灾祸？快走开。"

公主苏克拉坐在窗前，正在夕阳的余晖下读着浪漫的小说。

看到侍女捧着祭品站在门口，她惊得跳起身。

书从膝上掉下来，她对着斯丽马蒂低语："大胆女人，别去送死！"

斯丽马蒂走过一道道门。
她昂起头叫道："王宫的女人们，快出来！
拜佛的时刻已经来临啦！"
有的当面关门，有的张口大骂。
白昼最后一线余晖从王宫的青铜圆顶消逝。
深沉的阴影笼罩在街道的各个角落；城市的喧嚣沉寂；湿婆神庙的锣声宣告晚祷时辰来临。

秋日的黄昏如平静的湖面一样深沉，星光颤颤闪亮，王宫花园的卫兵透过树影，惊讶地发现佛陀神龛前亮起一排灯火。

他们拔出利剑奔去，叫道："什么人，蠢货，敢来找死？"

"我，斯丽马蒂，"她答道，声音甜美，"佛陀的奴婢。"
下一刻，她心口的血染红冰冷的大理石。
繁星寂静无语，神龛脚下最后一盏献祭的灯火终于熄灭了。

注：Bimbisâr，宾婆沙罗，古印度摩揭陀王国君主，信佛教。

44

The day that stands between you and me makes her last bow of farewell.

The night draws her veil over her face, and hides the one lamp burning in my chamber.

Your dark servant comes noiselessly and spreads the bridal carpet for you to take your seat there alone with me in the wordless silence till night is done.

你我间的白昼最后一次鞠躬，向我告辞。
夜晚蒙上她的面纱，也挡住了我屋内的那盏灯光。

你黝黑的仆人无声地走来，为你铺好婚毯，好让你我单独坐在无言寂静中，直至黑夜逝去。

45

My night has passed on the bed of sorrow, and my eyes are tired. My heavy heart is not yet ready to meet morning with its crowded joys.

Draw a veil over this naked light, beckon aside from me this glaring flash and dance of life.

Let the mantle of tender darkness cover me in its folds, and cover my pain awhile from the pressure of the world.

我的夜在悲痛之床度过，双眼困乏不已。我沉重的心没准备好迎接充满喜悦的清晨。

用面纱罩住赤裸灯光，引走我身边耀眼闪烁与生命之舞。

让温柔的黑斗篷把我罩在它褶缝中，让我的痛苦远离世界的压力片刻。

46

The time is past when I could repay her for all that I received.

Her night has found its morning and thou hast taken her to thy arms: and to thee I bring my gratitude and my gifts that were for her.

For all hurts and offences to her I come to thee for forgiveness.

I offer to thy service those flowers of my love that remained in bud when she waited for them to open.

我已错过报答她所有馈赠的最好时机。

她的夜晚找到清晨，你已把她拥入怀中；我将把我为她准备的感激和礼品给你。

我来找你，恳求你宽恕我对她的伤害和冒犯。

我把我的爱的鲜花也献给你，她曾苦等它们开放，却未能等到。

47

I found a few old letters of mine carefully hidden in her box—a few small toys for her memory to play with.

With a timorous heart she tried to steal these trifles from time's turbulent stream, and said, "These are mine only!"

Ah, there is no one now to claim them, who can pay their price with loving care, yet here they are still.

Surely there is love in this world to save her from utter loss, even like this love of hers that saved these letters with such fond care.

我发现她的盒子里珍藏着我的几封信，几个小玩具供她的记忆玩耍。

怀揣畏怯之心，她试图从时光湍流中偷走它们，说："它们只属于我！"

啊，现在无人要它们了，谁会付费照料它们？它们依旧在此。

这世上一定有爱存在，救她免于彻底失落，正像她的爱真情地把这些信保存下来。

48

Bring beauty and order into my forlorn life, woman, as you brought them into my house when you lived.

Sweep away the dusty fragments of the hours, fill the empty jars, and mend all that has been neglected.

Then open the inner door of the shrine, light the candle, and let us meet there in silence before our God.

女人，把美和秩序给我悲惨的生活，如你在世时带它们进我家。

请扫去时光的尘封碎屑，装满空水罐，修复曾被忽略的一切。

然后打开神殿的内大门，点燃蜡烛，让我们在神的面前静静相见。

49

The pain was great when the strings were being tuned, my Master!

Begin your music, and let me forget the pain; let me feel in beauty what you had in your mind through those pitiless days.

The waning night lingers at my doors, let her take her leave in songs.

Pour your heart into my life strings, my Master, in tunes that descend from your stars.

调校琴弦时痛苦实在大，我的神！

奏起你的乐曲，让我忘却痛苦；让我在美中感受你在无情的岁月中的心绪。

残夜仍逗留在我门口，让她在歌中道别。

伴着你的星曲，把你的心注入我命之弦，我的神。

50

In the lightning flash of a moment I have seen the immensity of your creation in my life—creation through many a death from world to world.

I weep at my unworthiness when I see my life in the hands of the unmeaning hours, —but when I see it in your hands I know it is too precious to be squandered among shadows.

在瞬间的雷鸣电闪中，我在我生命中看到你历经生死、从这世界到那世界的创造力的巨大。

看到我的生命握在虚空之中，我为我的毫无价值哭泣；当我见你把生命握手中，我知生命珍贵，不该浪费于暗影。

51

I know that at the dim end of some day the sun will bid me its farewell.

Shepherds will play their pipes beneath the banyan trees, and cattle graze on the slope by the river, while my days will pass into the dark.

This is my prayer, that I may know before I leave why the earth called me to her arms.

Why her night's silence spoke to me of stars, and her daylight kissed my thoughts into flower.

Before I go may I linger over my last refrain, completing its music, may the lamp be lit to see your face and the wreath woven to crown you.

我知道，有一天的暮色中太阳将会向我告别。

牧童将在榕树下面吹着风笛，牛群在河边的山坡吃草，而我的日子将进入黑暗。

我祈祷：我要知道，离去前，为何大地唤我去她的怀抱。

为何静夜给我讲星之事，为何白昼把我思绪吻成花。

让我离去前停留片刻，写出最后的副歌，谱完全曲；愿灯亮起好看到你的脸，织好花环为你加冕。

52

What music is that in whose measure the world is rocked?

We laugh when it beats upon the crest of life, we shrink in terror when it returns into the dark.

But the play is the same that comes and goes with the rhythm of the endless music.

You hide your treasure in the palm of your hand, and we cry that we are robbed.

But open and shut your palm as you will, the gain and the loss are the same.

At the game you play with your own self you lose and win at once.

那是何音乐，用其节拍摇撼世界？

它奏响在生命之巅，我们大笑，它返回黑暗时我们恐惧发抖。

但是随着无尽乐曲旋律的往复，演奏始终不变。

你把财富藏于掌心，我们叫嚷着：遭人抢劫了。

你随心所欲地松开或捏紧掌心，得失仍然相同。

你和自己玩着游戏，你同时又输又赢。

53

I have kissed this world with my eyes and my limbs; I have wrapt it within my heart in numberless folds; I have flooded its days and nights with thoughts till the world and my life have grown one, —and I love my life because I love the light of the sky so enwoven with me.

If to leave this world be as real as to love it—then there must be a meaning in the meeting and the parting of life.

If that love were deceived in death, then the canker of this deceit would eat into all things, and the stars would shrivel and grow black.

我用眼睛和四肢拥吻了这个世界；我把它层层包进我心里；我用思想淹没白天黑夜，直至世界和我的生命合而为一。我爱生命，因为我爱与我织为一体的光明。

如果离开这个世界与爱它一样真实，那么生命的聚散离合一定有深意。

若爱在被死亡欺骗，那么这欺骗的毒素会侵蚀万物，繁星也会枯萎，暗淡无光。

54

The Cloud said to me, "I vanish"; the Night said, "I plunge into the fiery dawn."

The Pain said, "I remain in deep silence as his footprint."

"I die into the fulness," said my life to me.

The Earth said, "My lights kiss your thoughts every moment."

"The days pass," Love said, "but I wait for you."

Death said, "I ply the boat of your life across the sea."

云对我说:"我要散去。"夜对我说:"我要投入火红黎明。"

痛苦对我说:"我保持静默,如他脚步。"

我的命对我说:"我要圆满死去。"

大地说:"我的光时刻吻你思想。"

爱情说:"时光流逝,我等你。"

死亡说:"我驾驶你生命之舟过海。"

55

Tulsidas, the poet, was wandering, deep in thought, by the Ganges, in that lonely spot where they burn their dead.

He found a woman sitting at the feet of the corpse of her dead husband, gaily dressed as for a wedding.

She rose as she saw him, bowed to him, and said, "Permit me, Master, with your blessing, to follow my husband to heaven."

"Why such hurry, my daughter?" asked Tulsidas. "Is not this earth also His who made heaven?"

"For heaven I do not long," said the woman. "I want my husband."

Tulsidas smiled and said to her, "Go back to your home, my child. Before the month is over you will find your husband."

The woman went back with glad hope. Tulsidas came to her every day and gave her high thoughts to think, till her heart was filled to the brim with divine love.

When the month was scarcely over, her neighbours came to her, asking, "Woman, have you found your husband?"

The widow smiled and said, "I have."

Eagerly they asked, "Where is he?"

"In my heart is my Lord, one with me," said the woman.

诗人杜尔西达斯漫步在恒河边焚烧死者的寂寞之处，陷入了沉思。

他发现一个妇女坐在丈夫尸体旁边，穿着如婚礼般的艳丽服装。

看见诗人她起身施礼，说道："大师，请赐福于我，让我跟随我的丈夫到天国去。"

"何必匆忙呀，孩子？"杜尔西达斯问，"人间不也是天帝所造？"

"我不向往天国，"妇人答道，"我只要我丈夫。"

杜尔西达斯笑道："回家吧，我的孩子。这个月底之前，你就会找到你丈夫。"

女人怀着热望回家，杜尔西达斯每天去看她，以高论促她思索，直到她的心中充满了神圣的爱。

快到月底了，邻居们都来看她，问道："女人，你找到你丈夫了吗？"

寡妇笑道："我找到了。"

他们急着问："在哪儿？"

"夫君在我心，与我一体。"女人答道。

注：Tulsidas，杜尔西达，1532—1623，古印度大诗人。

56

You came for a moment to my side and touched me with the great mystery of the woman that there is in the heart of creation.

She who is ever returning to God his own outflowing of sweetness; she is the ever fresh beauty and youth in nature; she dances in the bubbling streams and sings in the morning light; she with heaving waves suckles the thirsty earth; in her the Eternal One breaks in two in a joy that no longer may contain itself, and overflows in the pain of love.

你曾来到我身边，短暂陪伴我，用创世主心灵深处的女性的伟大奥秘触动了我。

她总以天帝自己源源不绝的甜美回报天帝；是自然界永远清新的美与青春；她在潺潺溪水中起舞，在晨光中歌唱；

用滚滚波涛哺育饥渴大地；在她身上，创世主一分为二，既有不再容易控制的欢乐，又洋溢着爱情的痛苦。

57

Who is she who dwells in my heart, the woman forlorn for ever?

I wooed her and I failed to win her.

I decked her with wreaths and sang in her praise.

A smile shone in her face for a moment, then it faded.

"I have no joy in thee," she cried, the woman in sorrow.

I bought her jewelled anklets and fanned her with a fan gem-studded; I made her a bed on a bedstead of gold.

There flickered a gleam of gladness in her eyes, then it died.

"I have no joy in these," she cried, the woman in sorrow.

I seated her upon a car of triumph and drove her from end to end of the earth.

Conquered hearts bowed down at her feet, and shouts of applause rang in the sky.

Pride shone in her eyes for a moment, then it was dimmed in tears.

"I have no joy in conquest," she cried, the woman in sorrow.

I asked her, "Tell me whom do you seek?"

She only said, "I wait for him of the unknown name."

Days pass by and she cries, "When will my beloved come whom I know not, and be known to me for ever?"

栖居我心中、永远孤独凄凉的女人是谁？

我追过她但没得到她。

我用花环装扮她，歌颂她。

她脸上笑意一闪而过，顷刻间便消失。

"在你这里我没欢乐。"忧伤的女人说。

我给她买宝石脚镯；我用宝扇为她扇风；我在金床架上为她铺床。

她眼中闪过一丝欢乐，但很快消失。

"在珠宝中我没欢乐。"忧伤的女人说。

我让她坐在凯旋之车上，驱车带她走遍世界各地。

被征服的心拜倒她脚下，欢呼声响彻云霄。

她眼中自豪瞬间一闪，很快在泪中消亡。

"在征服中我没欢乐。"忧伤的女人说。

我问她："告诉我，你找谁？"

她只是答："我等的人我不知其名。"

光阴荏苒，她喊道："我的至爱何时到？他不为我知又永为我知。"

58

Yours is the light that breaks forth from the dark, and the good that sprouts from the cleft heart of strife.

Yours is the house that opens upon the world, and the love that calls to the battlefield.

Yours is the gift that still is a gain when everything is a loss, and the life that flows through the caverns of death.

Yours is the heaven that lies in the common dust, and you are there for me, you are there for all.

你的光明从黑暗中迸发，你的美德从挣扎的心萌发。

你的房屋向世界敞开，你的深爱呼唤人们奔赴战场。

你的礼品是在万物皆失去时之所得，你的生命从死亡之穴中流出。

你的天堂坐落在平凡尘世间，你在那里，为我也为众人。

59

When the weariness of the road is upon me, and the thirst of the sultry day; when the ghostly hours of the dusk throw their shadows across my life, then I cry not for your voice only, my friend, but for your touch.

There is an anguish in my heart for the burden of its riches not given to you.

Put out your hand through the night, let me hold it and fill it and keep it; let me feel its touch along the lengthening stretch of my loneliness.

当我在路上疲惫不堪，酷热天气中干渴难忍之时，当黄昏时的幽灵把阴影投向我的生命，朋友，我渴望听到你的声音，得到你抚摸。

我的心痛苦万分，因为担着没把财富交给你的重负。

穿过黑夜，伸出手，让我握住它，塞满它，留住它；让我感到它抚摸时我不断延长的孤独。

60

The odour cries in the bud, "Ah me, the day departs, the happy day of spring, and I am a prisoner in petals!"

Do not lose heart, timid thing!

Your bonds will burst, the bud will open into flower, and when you die in the fulness of life, even then the spring will live on.

The odour pants and flutters within the bud, crying, "Ah me, the hours pass by, yet I do not know where I go, or what it is I seek!"

Do not lose heart, timid thing!

The spring breeze has overheard your desire, the day will not end before you have fulfilled your being.

Dark is the future to her, and the odour cries in despair, "Ah me, through whose fault is my life so unmeaning?

"Who can tell me, why I am at all?"

Do not lose heart, timid thing!

The perfect dawn is near when you will mingle your life with all life and know at last your purpose.

芬芳在蓓蕾里呼喊:"啊,一天过去,一个欢乐春日,而我却被囚禁在花瓣里!"

不要灰心,胆小鬼!

你的镣铐将断裂,蓓蕾将绽放花朵,即使你死于生命完美时刻,春光仍将继续。

芬芳在蓓蕾里喘息扑腾,大叫:"啊,时光飞逝,我却不知要去哪里,也不知我在寻求什么!"

不要灰心,胆小鬼!

和煦春风偷听到你心愿,今日未过,你就会实现生存目标。

她的将来一片黑暗,芬芳在绝望中叫:"啊,我的生命没意义,是谁的错?

"谁能告诉我,为何如此?"

不要灰心,胆小鬼!

完美黎明将近,你的生命与众生一体,你将知晓你的目的。

61

She is still a child, my Lord.

She runs about your palace and plays, and tries to make of you a plaything as well.

She heeds not when her hair tumbles down and her careless garment drags in the dust.

She falls asleep when you speak to her and answers not—and the flower you give her in the morning slips to the dust from her hands.

When the storm bursts and darkness is over the sky she is sleepless; her dolls lie scattered on the earth and she clings to you in terror.

She is afraid that she may fail in service to you.

But with a smile you watch her at her game.

You know her.

The child sitting in the dust is your destined bride; her play will be stilled and deepened into love.

神啊，她还是孩子。

她在你宫殿奔跑嬉戏，还想把你也变成她的玩具。

她不在意头发散乱，随便穿的衣裙拖在尘土里。

你和她说话，她酣然入睡，不回话——早晨你送给她的鲜花从她的手中滑落在地。

风狂雨骤，黑暗笼罩天空，她的睡意全无，玩偶散落在地，她惊恐地紧紧依偎着你。

她担心自己不能很好地服侍你。

你却微笑看着她玩游戏。

你懂她。

地上的女孩是你命定的新娘；她停止嬉戏，化作深深爱意。

62

"What is there but the sky, O Sun, that can hold thine image?"

"I dream of thee, but to serve thee I can never hope," the dewdrop wept and said, "I am too small to take thee unto me, great Lord, and my life is all tears."

"I illumine the limitless sky, yet I can yield myself up to a tiny drop of dew," thus the Sun said; "I shall become but a sparkle of light and fill you, and your little life will be a laughing orb."

"啊，太阳，除天空，有谁能容纳你形象？"

"我梦见你，但从不奢望侍奉你。"露珠哭道，"我太渺小承受不住，伟大的神，我的生命全是泪珠。"

于是太阳说："我照亮无垠的天空，但也能屈尊于一滴微小的露珠。我将化为闪光填满你。这样，你的小生命将成为含笑的天体。"

63

Not for me is the love that knows no restraint, but like the foaming wine that having burst its vessel in a moment would run to waste.

Send me the love which is cool and pure like your rain that blesses the thirsty earth and fills the homely earthen jars.

Send me the love that would soak down into the centre of being, and from there would spread like the unseen sap through the branching tree of life, giving birth to fruits and flowers.

Send me the love that keeps the heart still with the fulness of peace.

没有节制的爱不适合于我，它像冒泡的汽酒，顷刻间从酒瓶里溢出来就变为废物。

赐给我清凉纯净的爱，像雨水一样赐福干渴大地，注满朴素的陶罐。

赐给我能够渗透入心灵深处的爱，像那看不见的树液从那里流遍生命之树的枝叶，结出鲜花和果实。

赐给我使心灵平静、充满平和的爱吧。

64

The sun had set on the western margin of the river among the tangle of the forest.

The hermit boys had brought the cattle home, and sat round the fire to listen to the master, Guatama, when a strange boy came, and greeted him with fruits and flowers, and, bowing low at his feet, spoke in a bird-like voice—"Lord, I have come to thee to be taken into the path of the supreme Truth.

"My name is Satyakâma."

"Blessings be on thy head," said the master.

"Of what clan art thou, my child? It is only fitting for a Brahmin to aspire to the highest wisdom."

"Master," answered the boy, "I know not of what clan I am. I shall go and ask my mother."

Thus saying, Satyakâma took leave, and wading across the shallow stream, came back to his mother's hut, which stood at the end of the sandy waste at the edge of the sleeping village.

The lamp burnt dimly in the room, and the mother stood at the door in the dark waiting for her son's return.

She clasped him to her bosom, kissed him on his hair, and asked him of his errand to the master.

"What is the name of my father, dear mother?" asked the boy.

"It is only fitting for a Brahmin to aspire to the highest wisdom, said Lord Guatama to me."

The woman lowered her eyes, and spoke in a whisper.

"In my youth I was poor and had many masters. Thou didst come to thy mother Jabâlâ's arms, my darling, who had no husband."

The early rays of the sun glistened on the tree-tops of the forest hermitage.

The students, with their tangled hair still wet with their morning bath, sat under the ancient tree, before the master.

There came Satyakâma.

He bowed low at the feet of the sage, and stood silent.

"Tell me," the great teacher asked him, "of what clan art thou?"

"My Lord," he answered, "I know it not. My mother said when I asked her, 'I had served many masters in my youth, and thou hadst come to thy mother Jabâlâ's arms, who had no husband.'"

There rose a murmur like the angry hum of bees disturbed in their hive; and the students muttered at the shameless insolence of that outcast.

Master Guatama rose from his seat, stretched out his arms, took the boy to his bosom, and said, "Best of all Brahmins art thou, my child. Thou hast the noblest heritage of truth."

太阳已经落在蜿蜒于枝繁叶茂的密林中一条河的西岸。

隐修院的孩子放牧归来，围坐炉火边倾听大师乔达摩讲经。一个陌生少年手捧水果鲜花走来向大师致敬，拜伏在他脚下，鸟语般地说："大师，我来拜您为师，请您引我走上至高的真理之路。

"我名叫沙笃伽姆。"

"愿福佑降临于你。"大师道。

"孩子，你属于什么种姓？只有婆罗门种姓的人才配追求最高的智慧。"

"大师，"少年答道，"我不知道我的种姓，我要去问我的母亲。"

说罢，沙笃伽姆转身离开，他蹚过浅浅的小溪，回到母亲的小屋。小屋坐落在沉睡的村庄边一片荒沙地的尽头。

屋内点着昏暗的灯，母亲伫立在门口的黑暗中，等待儿子的归来。

她把儿子紧搂入怀，亲吻着他的头发，询问他拜师的情况。

"妈妈呀，我的父亲姓什么？"孩子问。

"乔达摩大师对我说道，只有婆罗门种姓的人才配追求最高的智慧。"

妇人双眼低垂，声音低如耳语：

"我年轻时很穷，侍奉过许多主人。宝贝，你来到妈妈查芭拉怀里时，她没有丈夫。"

初升太阳的光辉在隐修院的树梢上闪闪发着光。

弟子们晨浴完毕，蓬乱的头发湿漉漉的，在古树下，坐在大师面前。

沙笃伽姆走来。

他伏在圣人的脚前，深深鞠躬。

"告诉我，"大师道，"你属于什么种姓？"

"大师，"少年答道，"我不知道。我问过母亲了，她说：'我年轻时很穷，侍奉过许多主人。你来到妈妈查芭拉怀里时，她没有丈夫。'"

嗡嗡声起，如蜜蜂受惊，在蜂箱里愤怒鸣叫，弟子们咕哝着指责这个贱民的厚颜无耻。

大师乔达摩从座位站起，伸开双臂，搂少年在怀里："孩子，你是最高贵的婆罗门。你守住最高尚的真实。"

65

Maybe there is one house in this city where the gate opens for ever this morning at the touch of the sunrise, where the errand of the light is fulfilled.

The flowers have opened in hedges and gardens, and may be there is one heart that has found in them this morning the gift that has been on its voyage from endless time.

也许在这个城市里有一座房子，今晨在朝阳的抚慰下永远敞开大门，光明的使命由此完成。

树篱和花园中鲜花盛开，也许有一颗心已经发现，就在今晨，无穷的时光送来的礼品已经在路上。

66

Listen, my heart, in his flute is the music of the smell of wild flowers, of the glistening leaves and gleaming water, of shadows resonant with bees' wings.

The flute steals his smile from my friend's lips and spreads it over my life.

我的心，听，他的笛声中有野花的芬芳、闪光的绿叶和闪亮的碧水，还有回响着蜜蜂振翅的浓荫。

长笛在我朋友唇边偷笑，融入我的生命。

67

You always stand alone beyond the stream of my songs.

The waves of my tunes wash your feet but I know not how to reach them.

This play of mine with you is a play from afar.

It is the pain of separation that melts into melody through my flute.

I wait for the time when your boat crosses over to my shore and you take my flute into your own hands.

你总独自站在我歌曲之河彼岸。

歌波冲着我不知怎样抵达的你的双脚。

我和你的这场游戏相隔遥远。

分离的痛苦通过我的长笛熔成了悦耳的音调。

我等待你的小船驶过河面，来到我的岸边，双手拿过我的长笛。

68

Suddenly the window of my heart flew open this morning, the window that looks out on your heart.

I wondered to see that the name by which you know me is written in April leaves and flowers, and I sat silent.

The curtain was blown away for a moment between my songs and yours.

I found that your morning light was full of my own mute songs unsung; I thought that I would learn them at your feet—and I sat silent.

今天清晨，我的心灵之窗突然打开，那朝向你的心灵之窗。

我惊奇地看到，你所知的我的名字写在四月的花叶之上，我默默坐下。

你我歌声之间的帘子刹那间就被吹走。

我发现你的晨光充满我沉默未唱的歌；我该在你足下学唱它们——我默默坐下。

69

You were in the centre of my heart, therefore when my heart wandered she never found you; you hid yourself from my loves and hopes till the last, for you were always in them.

You were the inmost joy in the play of my youth, and when I was too busy with the play the joy was passed by.

You sang to me in the ecstasies of my life and I forgot to sing to you.

你在我的内心深处，因此我的心徘徊时，她无法发现你；你始终躲避我的爱与希望，因为你一直在它们之中。

你是我青春游戏最深的欢乐，每当我沉溺于游戏中，欢乐就会消失。

你在我生命狂喜时对我歌唱，可我忘了为你歌唱。

70

When you hold your lamp in the sky it throws its light on my face and its shadow falls over you.

When I hold the lamp of love in my heart its light falls on you and I am left standing behind in the shadow.

你把灯举到空中，灯光洒在我脸上，而阴影却落在你身上。

你在我心中举起爱情之灯，灯光落在你身上，我却在后面的阴影中。

71

O the waves, the sky-devouring waves, glistening with light, dancing with life, the waves of eddying joy, rushing for ever.

The stars rock upon them, thoughts of every tint are cast up out of the deep and scattered on the beach of life.
Birth and death rise and fall with their rhythm, and the sea-gull of my heart spreads its wings crying in delight.

啊，波浪，吞噬天空的波浪，光芒闪耀，与生命共舞，快乐旋转的波浪，奔流永不息。

星星在波浪上摇摆，五彩思绪从海底涌出，被抛撒在生命的海滩。

生与死随节奏起伏不定，我心灵的海鸥舒展翅膀，快乐地鸣唱。

72

The joy ran from all the world to build my body.

The lights of the skies kissed and kissed her till she woke.

Flowers of hurrying summers sighed in her breath and voices of winds and water sang in her movements.

The passion of the tide of colours in clouds and in forests flowed into her life, and the music of all things caressed her limbs into shape.

She is my bride, —she has lighted her lamp in my house.

欢乐从世界各地来打造我身体。

天之光一遍遍亲她直到她醒来。

匆匆夏日的鲜花跟她一起叹息，风声水声随着她的运动歌唱。

云和林中潮水般的五彩激情注入她的生命，万物的音乐声轻抚她的四肢使之成形。

她是我的新娘，——在我家点亮了灯光。

73

The spring with its leaves and flowers has come into my body.

The bees hum there the morning long, and the winds idly play with the shadows.

A sweet fountain springs up from the heart of my heart.

My eyes are washed with delight like the dew-bathed morning, and life is quivering in all my limbs like the sounding strings of the lute.

Are you wandering alone by the shore of my life, where the tide is in flood, O lover of my endless days?

Are my dreams flitting round you like the moths with their many-coloured wings?

And are those your songs that are echoing in the dark eaves of my being?

Who but you can hear the hum of the crowded hours that sounds in my veins to-day, the glad steps that dance in my breast, the clamour of the restless life beating its wings in my body?

春天带着绿叶鲜花进入我的生命。

清晨，蜜蜂嗡嗡不停，春风懒懒地和绿荫嬉戏。

一股蜜泉从我内心深处涌出。

我的双眼被喜悦洗净，如朝露沐浴的早晨；生命在我四肢颤动，如振响的琴弦。

啊，我无限时光的爱人，是你在我浪潮汹涌的生命岸边独自徘徊吗？

是我的梦想如彩翅的飞蛾在围着你飞翔吗？

是你的歌声在我存在的黑暗洞穴中回荡吗？

除了你，谁能听见今天在我脉搏里喧闹时光的嗡嗡声，胸口上轻快的舞步，以及我体内躁动生命振翅的喧闹？

74

My bonds are cut, my debts are paid, my door has been opened, I go everywhere.

They crouch in their corner and weave their web of pale hours, they count their coins sitting in the dust and call me back.

But my sword is forged, my armour is put on, my horse is eager to run.

I shall win my kingdom.

锁链已断，债务已还，大门已开，我将要奔向四方。

他们缩在角落编织苍白时间之网，他们坐在尘埃中数钱，唤我归来。

我的剑已铸好，盔甲已披上身，战马渴望奔驰。

我要赢回王国。

75

It was only the other day that I came to your earth, naked and nameless, with a wailing cry.

To-day my voice is glad, while you, my Lord, stand aside to make room that I may fill my life.

Even when I bring you my songs for an offering I have the secret hope that men will come and love me for them.

You love to discover that I love this world where you have brought me.

不久之前我来到你的大地，赤身裸体，无名无姓，哇地一声叫。

今天，我声音欢快，你，我的神，闪一边，腾出空间充实我生命。

当我向你献歌时我也暗自希望，这些歌能引世人来交换对我的爱。

你会乐见，我热爱你带我来的这个世界。

76

Timidly I cowered in the shadow of safety, but now, when the surge of joy carries my heart upon its crest, my heart clings to the cruel rock of its trouble.

I sat alone in a corner of my house thinking it too narrow for any guest, but now when its door is flung open by an unbidden joy I find there is room for thee and for all the world.

I walked upon tiptoe, careful of my person, perfumed, and adorned—but now when a glad whirlwind has overthrown me in the dust I laugh and roll on the earth at thy feet like a child.

　　我曾胆怯地蜷缩在安全阴影中；现在，喜悦的波浪把我的心推到浪尖，我的心紧抓烦恼残忍的礁石。

　　独坐家中一角我想，房子窄小无法容下任何来客；现在，门被未请自来的欢乐撞开，我发现它能容下你，容下整个世界。

　　我踮脚行走，留神我精心打扮馥郁的身姿；现在，当幸福旋风把我卷入尘土中，我像个孩子在你脚下的地面翻滚。

77

The world is yours at once and for ever.

And because you have no want, my king, you have no pleasure in your wealth.

It is as though it were naught.

Therefore through slow time you give me what is yours, and ceaselessly win your kingdom in me.

Day after day you buy your sunrise from my heart, and you find your love carven into the image of my life.

　　世界属于你，永远属于你。
　　因你从无匮乏，我的王，财富不会给你欢乐。

你视财富如无物。

经年累月你把你的给我，自我你不停赢取你的王国。

日复一日，你从我心中买到日出，你发现你的爱塑成我生命的形象。

78

To the birds you gave songs, the birds gave you songs in return.

You gave me only voice, yet asked for more, and I sing.

You made your winds light and they are fleet in their service. You burdened my hands that I myself may lighten them, and at last, gain unburdened freedom for your service.

You created your Earth filling its shadows with fragments of light.

There you paused; you left me empty-handed in the dust to create your heaven.

To all things else you give; from me you ask.

The harvest of my life ripens in the sun and the shower till I reap more than you sowed, gladdening your heart, O Master of the golden granary.

你把歌赐予鸟，鸟以歌回赠于你。

你只赐我歌喉，要的却多，我歌唱。

你赐风轻盈，风快速地为你忙碌。你使我双手负担沉重，让我自己减负，卸去负担，自由地为你服务。

你造出你的大地，用光明碎片塞满阴影。

你停下，剩我两手空空，在尘土上建造你的天堂。

你给予众生；对我只是索取。

阳光雨露中我生命的作物成熟，直到我的收成多于你的播种，令你心中充满欢喜，噢，金色谷仓之主。

79

Let me not pray to be sheltered from dangers but to be fearless in facing them.

Let me not beg for the stilling of my pain but for the heart to conquer it.

Let me not look for allies in life's battlefield but to my own strength.

Let me not crave in anxious fear to be saved but hope for the patience to win my freedom.

Grant me that I may not be a coward, feeling your mercy in my success alone; but let me find the grasp of your hand in my failure.

别让我祈祷免遭危险，而让我无畏惧地面对危险。

别让我祈求消除痛苦，而让我有征服痛苦的心。

别让我在生命战场寻友，而让我自己有力。

别让我在焦虑恐惧中求救，而让我希冀耐心赢得自由。

答应我，别让我成为懦夫，只在成功时感知你仁慈；而让我失败时找到你紧握的双手。

80

You did not know yourself when you dwelt alone, and there was no crying of an errand when the wind ran from the hither to the farther shore.

I came and you woke, and the skies blossomed with lights.

You made me open in many flowers; rocked me in the cradles of many forms; hid me in death and found me again in life.

I came and your heart heaved; pain came to you and joy.
You touched me and tingled into love.

But in my eyes there is a film of shame and in my breast a
flicker of fear; my face is veiled and I weep when I cannot see
you.

Yet I know the endless thirst in your heart for sight of me,
the thirst that cries at my door in the repeated knockings of
sunrise.

独居时，你并不了解你自己，当风从此岸吹向遥远的彼
岸之时，没有传来任务的呼唤。

我来，你醒来，霞光之花开满天。
是你让我在花中绽放；用各种摇篮摇我入睡；你藏我在
死中，又在生中找回我。

我来了，你心潮起伏，又悲又喜。
你抚摩我，爱意在震颤。

我的眼中露出一层羞涩，胸口闪现出一丝恐惧；脸埋面
纱中，没看见你，我哭起来。

我知道，你的心无比渴望与我会面，这渴望伴随着朝霞在不断叩响我的大门。

81

You, in your timeless watch, listen to my approaching steps while your gladness gathers in the morning twilight and breaks in the burst of light.

The nearer I draw to you the deeper grows the fervour in the dance of the sea.

Your world is a branching spray of light filling your hands, but your heaven is in my secret heart; it slowly opens its buds in shy love.

在无尽守望中，你倾听着我渐进脚步。你的欢乐在晨曦中聚集，骤然喷出道道霞光。

我和你离得越近，大海狂舞的热烈就越来越深沉。

你的世界是你手中分叉的光枝，你的天国在我秘密的心里；它在羞爱之中徐徐绽开。

82

I will utter your name, sitting alone among the shadows of my silent thoughts.

I will utter it without words, I will utter it without purpose.
For I am like a child that calls its mother a hundred times, glad that it can say "Mother."

在无言思绪的阴影中独坐时，我会喊出你的名字。

喊出你的名字，不需要言辞，也无任何目的。
因为我像孩子，一次次喊着母亲，为自己会叫"母亲"开心。

83

I
I feel that all the stars shine in me.
The world breaks into my life like a flood.
The flowers blossom in my body.

All the youthfulness of land and water smokes like an incense in my heart; and the breath of all things plays on my thoughts as on a flute.

II

When the world sleeps I come to your door.

The stars are silent, and I am afraid to sing.

I wait and watch, till your shadow passes by the balcony of night and I return with a full heart.

Then in the morning I sing by the roadside;

The flowers in the hedge give me answer and the morning air listens,

The travellers suddenly stop and look in my face, thinking I have called them by their names.

III

Keep me at your door ever attending to your wishes, and let me go about in your Kingdom accepting your call.

Let me not sink and disappear in the depth of languor.

Let not my life be worn out to tatters by penury of waste.

Let not those doubts encompass me, —the dust of distractions.

Let me not pursue many paths to gather many things.

Let me not bend my heart to the yoke of the many.

Let me hold my head high in the courage and pride of being your servant.

I

感觉群星在我心中闪。

世界如洪流涌进我生命。

百花在我的体内绽放。

大地和水的全部朝气像香烛在我心中冒起；万物的气息如长笛吹拂我的思绪。

II

世界沉睡，我来到你门口。

繁星静默不语，我也不敢歌唱。

我等待观望，直至你的身影掠过夜的阳台，我才心满意足地返回。

待到黎明时，我在路边歌唱；

篱笆内的花朵纷纷回应，清晨空气也在听。

旅人突然停下，看着我的脸庞，以为我叫他们的名字。

III

把我留在你的门边，随时听你差遣，让我接受你的召唤，在你的王国游走。

别让我在倦怠的深渊里沉没消失。

别让荒芜的匮乏把我的生命撕成碎片。

别让那些疑虑把我笼罩——分神的尘埃。

别让我探查聚敛金钱财物的门路。

别让我违心屈从于多数人支配。

让我以做你仆人的勇气自豪地把头高高昂起。

84

The Oarsman

Do you hear the tumult of death afar,

The call midst the fire-floods and poisonous clouds

—The Captain's call to the steersman to turn the ship to an unnamed shore,

For that time is over—the stagnant time in the port—

Where the same old merchandise is bought and sold in an endless round,

Where dead things drift in the exhaustion and emptiness of truth.

They wake up in sudden fear and ask,

"Comrades, what hour has struck?

When shall the dawn begin?"

The clouds have blotted away the stars—

Who is there then can see the beckoning finger of the day?

They run out with oars in hand, the beds are emptied, the mother prays, the wife watches by the door;

There is a wail of parting that rises to the sky,

And there is the Captain's voice in the dark:

"Come, sailors, for the time in the harbour is over!"

All the black evils in the world have overflowed their banks,

Yet, oarsmen, take your places with the blessing of sorrow in your souls!

Whom do you blame, brothers? Bow your heads down!

The sin has been yours and ours.

The heat growing in the heart of God for ages—

The cowardice of the weak, the arrogance of the strong, the greed of fat prosperity, the rancour of the wronged, pride of race, and insult to man—

Has burst God's peace, raging in storm.

Like a ripe pod, let the tempest break its heart into pieces, scattering thunders.

Stop your bluster of dispraise and of self-praise,

And with the calm of silent prayer on your foreheads sail to that unnamed shore.

We have known sins and evils every day and death we have known;

They pass over our world like clouds mocking us with their transient lightning laughter.

Suddenly they have stopped, become a prodigy,

And men must stand before them saying:

"We do not fear you, O Monster! for we have lived every day by conquering you,

"And we die with the faith that Peace is true, and Good is true, and true is the eternal One!"

If the Deathless dwell not in the heart of death,

If glad wisdom bloom not bursting the sheath of sorrow,

If sin do not die of its own revealment,

If pride break not under its load of decorations,

Then whence comes the hope that drives these men from their homes like stars rushing to their death in the morning light?

Shall the value of the martyrs' blood and mothers' tears be utterly lost in the dust of the earth, not buying Heaven with their price?

And when Man bursts his mortal bounds, is not the Boundless revealed that moment?

划桨手

你听见远方死亡的喧闹，
那火海和毒云间传来的呼叫
——是船长在命令舵手把船转向无名的海岸，
时间已经过去——港口停滞的时间
那里，同样的老货买卖在无止境地循环，
那里，死物飘浮在真实枯竭空虚之中。

他们从惊恐中突醒，问：
"伙伴们，几点钟了？
黎明何时到来？"
滚滚乌云遮住了群星——
谁能够看见白天在频频招手的手指？

他们拿桨跑出来，床空了，母亲在祈祷，妻子在门边
观望；
一阵离别的痛哭之声冲上天空。
黑暗中传来船长的呼喊：
"水手们，起航，没时间待在港口啦！"

世上所有黑色邪恶都已漫过堤岸，
桨手们，各就各位，在灵魂中藏起悲伤祝福！
弟兄们，能怪谁？低下头吧！
这是你我大家的罪。

天帝心中热火已积聚多年——

弱者的胆怯、强者的傲慢、富贵者的贪婪、冤屈者的怨恨、种族的骄傲以及人类承受的侮辱——

怒吼冲破天帝平静。

让暴风像成熟豆荚撕碎自己的心，化作四散雷霆。

闭嘴，别诽谤他人，吹嘘自己。

带着额上无言祈祷的寂静，驶向那无名的彼岸。

我们每天遇见罪孽与邪恶，遭遇死亡；

它们像乌云飘过世界，以闪电般的狂笑嘲弄我们。

它们突然停下，变成庞然奇物。

人们必须站其面前说：

"我们不怕你，噢，妖魔！因为征服你我们活过每一天，即使死去，信念仍坚：和平是真，善是真，永恒之子也是真！"

如果永生不居于死亡之心，

如果愉快智慧不从悲之鞘绽放，

如果罪恶不死于自我暴露，

如果骄傲没在虚饰重负下压倒，

让桨手们如繁星在曙光中奔向死亡离家的希望来自哪里？

难道殉难者的血和母亲的泪完全丧失在大地尘埃中，如此代价也买不了上天？

凡人挣脱尘世束缚，正是无束之帝显灵之时？

85

The Song of the Defeated

My Master has bid me while I stand at the roadside, to sing the song of Defeat, for that is the bride whom He woos in secret.

She has put on the dark veil, hiding her face from the crowd, but the jewel glows on her breast in the dark.

She is forsaken of the day, and God's night is waiting for her with its lamps lighted and flowers wet with dew.

She is silent with her eyes downcast; she has left her home behind her, from her home has come that wailing in the wind.

But the stars are singing the love-song of the eternal to a face sweet with shame and suffering.

The door has been opened in the lonely chamber, the call has sounded, and the heart of the darkness throbs with awe because of the coming tryst.

致失败者们的歌

我伫立在路边，主人吩咐我唱一支失败之歌，因为失败是他暗中追求的新娘。

她蒙上黑纱，不让人群见她的脸，她胸前的宝石在黑暗中闪光。

她被白昼所遗弃，天帝的夜晚用点亮的灯和露珠滋润的花朵着她。

她低垂双眼，默默无语；她把家抛之身后，夜风里从她家中传来哀哭。

面对因羞涩痛苦而变得甜美的脸，繁星唱起一支永恒恋歌。

寂寞密室房门已开，召唤之声已经响起，对即将来临的幽会黑暗之心因敬畏而悸动。

86

Thanksgiving

Those who walk on the path of pride crushing the lowly life under their tread, covering the tender green of the earth with their footprints in blood;

Let them rejoice, and thank thee, Lord, for the day is theirs.

But I am thankful that my lot lies with the humble who suffer and bear the burden of power, and hide their faces and stifle their sobs in the dark.

For every throb of their pain has pulsed in the secret depth of thy night, and every insult has been gathered into thy great silence. And the morrow is theirs.

O Sun, rise upon the bleeding hearts blossoming in flowers of the morning, and the torchlight revelry of pride shrunken to ashes.

感恩曲

行走在傲慢路上的人，践踏着卑贱者的生命，他们沾满鲜血的足迹踏遍大地的嫩绿。

让他们狂欢，今天归他们，神，多谢。

我要感谢你，让我的命运与卑贱者一起，他们受苦，忍受权势压迫，在黑暗中掩面强忍眼泪。

他们每一次阵痛都在你夜的秘密深处震颤，每一次侮辱都汇入你宏大的沉默。明天属于他们。

啊，太阳，从滴血的心灵上升起，绽放出黎明之花，让傲慢的火炬狂欢皱缩化为灰烬。

译后记

　　接触泰戈尔的《飞鸟集》，是在我读大学之时。那时，"文革"刚刚结束，我有幸成为其后第一届跨入大学的 77级学生，来到了西南地区知名学府四川大学，进入外文系英文专业学习，终于成为名副其实的大学生。我最初读到的是郑振铎的中译本，当时就被泰戈尔那清新瑰丽的小诗和郑先生的优美译文所感动。世界文豪在《飞鸟集》中用 300 多首简短的小诗为我们展现了大自然的美景、母亲对孩子的慈爱、青年男女之间纯真的爱情、朋友之间的真挚友情。郑振铎先生用浅显易懂的白话文为我们呈现了大师发自内心的对大自然、对人类的无限深情，其中有些诗句至今令我难以忘怀：

　　"使生如夏花之绚烂，死如秋叶之静美。"

　　"荣誉羞着我，因为我暗地里求着它。"

　　"绿草求她地上的伴侣，树木求他天空的寂寞。"

"夜秘密地把花开放了，却让那白日去领受谢词。"

在毕业前夕，我又读到了《飞鸟集》的英文版。这时我发现，这些短诗的英语所用的单词并不多。英语不是泰戈尔的母语，他的诗歌大都是他后来用英语翻译的，但也有些诗歌是直接用英语写就的。和郑振铎先生的译文对照而读，我发现郑先生的译文是将近100年前的白话文，和当代汉语的差别已不是一星半点，有必要重译。因此我萌发了重译《飞鸟集》的想法。

然而，1982年1月毕业后，我被分配到一所工科大学（当时名叫重庆交通学院），从事大学英语教学工作，我的文学梦就戛然而止。翻译工作是做过的，但那是科技翻译——我曾为钱伟长任主编的《应用数学和力学》（月刊，中英文版在国内外同时出版发行）审读论文长达8年，合计审读了大约2000万字。11年之后的1993年，我调到了浙江大学，曾打算重拾文学研究和文学翻译之梦，但是出于工作原因，我的文学梦依然遥遥无期。退休以后，总算有了闲暇，可以做点自己想做的事。文学之梦再次燃起。当然，作诗写小说的激情早已不在。不过，几十年的英语教学与研究，以及后来同时从事的汉语国际教育的教学与研究，为我的翻译实践奠定了坚实的基础。于是，我开始翻译一些英美诗人的短诗，凑成两本——《美诗佳韵》和《英诗佳韵》，现已出版。

其间，我又拿起了泰戈尔的《飞鸟集》，还找到了他的其他几本短诗集，发现它们都是很短的散文诗合集。考虑到篇幅，遂决定把《飞鸟集》《流萤集》与《采果集》翻译出来，合集出版。

《飞鸟集》的一部分（大约30%），就是100余首（第51—160首），以及《采果集》的一部分（大约30%），就是20余首（第61—86首），由湖南大学的黄尚戎翻译。他虽是计算机专业出身，但在德国和澳大利亚留学、工作10余年，拿到了硕士和博士学位。在国外学习和工作期间，英语一直是他的工作语言，他的专业论文均为英语写就并在国外相关领域的重要学术杂志发表。目前，他在从事大数据的研究，计算机翻译也是他涉猎的一个重要领域；他还在指导研究生从事英汉诗歌的计算机翻译研究，即将有一本机器翻译的现当代汉语的英译诗歌集出版。泰戈尔英文诗歌的语言对他来说没有什么压力。当然他译的部分，我也进行了一些文字上的校订。

本书的翻译采用"字数相应"译法中的最初模式，即"字数相等译法"，也就是一个英语音节用一个汉字译出，完全按照"1∶1"的方式翻译英语诗歌，这样可以达到一音对一音的效果，让读者在一定程度上感受到英语诗歌节奏之美。前辈诗歌翻译大师如朱湘、戴镏龄、施颖洲、高健等都曾用这一方法翻译过一些英美诗歌。

采用"字数相等译法"，可以在视觉上还原英诗的形式美。但是，英诗的格律和汉语诗歌有各自的特点。汉语以字为单位。汉语诗歌每行的字数从上古的二言体、三言体发展到《诗经》的四言体，之后发展到唐代以五言体和七言体（二字音组或三字音组）为主。而词曲则继承了《楚辞》的口语化节奏体系，不限顿的字数（顿的音节容量增多加大），不限诗行的音节数。（许霆：《中国新诗的韵律节奏论》，北京师范大学出版社，2016）英语以音节为单位，构成英诗的节奏的基础是韵律（metre），各行讲究一定的音节数量。英语的诗句，按音节和重音计算韵律，度量韵律的单位为音步（foot）。每个音步由一个重读音节和一个或多个非重读音节构成。重读音节为扬，非重读音节为抑，在英诗中按规律交替出现。英诗中的音步常用的有：抑扬格、扬抑格、扬抑抑格、抑扬抑格等，由此产生英诗的节奏美。诗行的长短以音步数目计算，有单音步诗、二音步诗、三音步诗、四音步诗，甚至八音步诗等。（罗良功：《英诗概论》，武汉大学出版社，2002）这样，每行的音节数可以是二到十甚至二十多不等。

由于汉诗和英诗的节奏韵律并不相同，因此，完全按照"1:1"的方式翻译英语诗歌，也只能在一定程度上体现英语诗歌的节奏韵律。这种译法，也无法顾及英诗的音步，难以体现英诗的轻重音以表现其抑扬顿挫之感。另外，英诗往往用词精练，单音节词居多，早期英诗更是如此，甚至有的英诗每行都是单音节词，这样的诗句往往很难完全按照"1:1"的方式翻译。尽管如此，我们还是坚持完全按照"1:1"的方式翻译英诗，以求在一定程度上为读者还原英诗的节奏韵律之美。因此，本书的书名也同样采用此译法。当然，由于泰戈尔用词简单，多音节词很少，大部分是单音节词和双音节词，完全按照"1:1"的方式以当代汉语翻译，其难度比英诗、美诗，尤其是美诗要大很多，但是我们仍坚守初衷，勉力而为。

押韵和节奏一样，是诗歌的基本特征之一，可以表现诗歌的音乐性。押韵可以使诗歌容易朗读和背诵，使诗歌流畅，

391

富有韵味。(聂珍钊:《英语诗歌形式导论》,中国社会科学出版社,2007)由于汉英语音系统的不同,英诗的一些音韵形式在汉语中很难表现出来,如英诗中行中韵里的头韵(alliteration)、元韵(assonance)和辅韵(consonance)。英诗和汉诗类似的是尾韵(end rhyme),但其格式也不尽相同。不过,泰戈尔的《飘鸟》《萤火虫》和《采果之歌》都是很短的散文诗,是无韵诗,基本上没有押韵的问题。本书对押韵并不做过多考虑,只要读来朗朗上口即可。

诗歌是一种特殊的文学形式,其意义很难从构筑诗歌的文字符号的字面上去理解。诗歌的意义可以分为三个层次:字面意义、感官意义和情感意义。中国有"诗言志""诗者,吟咏性情也"等的说法,英语诗歌,当然也不例外。英国诗人济慈说,"诗的生命在于热情";另一位英国诗人柯勒律治则指出,"诗歌是再现自然环境和人类思想感情的艺术"。诗歌意义的表现形式主要有:模糊、反语、似是而非。(罗良功:《英诗概论》,武汉大学出版社,2002)美国诗人弗罗斯特则认为:"隐喻,即指东说西,以此述彼,隐秘的欢欣。诗简直几首由隐喻构成。……每首诗在其本质上都是一个新的隐喻,不然就什么都不是。"(弗罗斯特:《弗罗斯特集:诗全集、散文和戏剧作品》,曹明伦译,辽宁教育出版社,2002)因此,在翻译中,要准确地表达原作者的本意是很难的。也正因为如此,才有弗罗斯特的名言:诗歌是翻译后失去的东西。尽管诗歌翻译很难,但是,为了不同国家和民族的人们欣赏和体味其他国家和民族的优秀诗歌作品,历代译者仍然不遗余力地在诗歌翻译领域艰难跋涉。本书在翻译的时候，也尽力还原作者的本意。希望这一努力能够得到读者的认同。

《飘鸟》在市面上有多种译本，书名均为《飞鸟集》。本书选择了《飘鸟》作为书名，既体现了"字数相等"的理念，也还原了泰戈尔的本意，更为传神。根据 *The New Oxford Dictionary of English*《新牛津英语词典》（1998），作为形容词的 stray 在修饰动物时的意思为：

> (of a domestic animal) having no home or having wandered away from home: stray dogs.

stray birds 中的 stray 表示"走失的、走散的、无主的、离群的"，即"飘，随风飞扬，飘（漂）泊"之意，因此 stray birds 可以译为"飘鸟"或"漂鸟"。

另外，《萤火虫》采用了直译的方法，《采果集》改为《采果之歌》。

泰戈尔的《飘鸟》英文版为326首，但其中第98首和第263首相同，故删除原第263首，实际为325首。

本书将泰戈尔《飘鸟》和《萤火虫》的中译文改为分行排列的方式，更加体现了诗歌的形式美，从视觉和听觉（诵读时）的角度给读者以更加愉悦的美的享受。

我们在翻译《飘鸟》时，参考了郑振铎、王钦刚、胡德夫、陆晋德和刘育琳的译文；在翻译《萤火虫》时，参考了吴岩、李家真、王钦刚和孙达的译文；在翻译《采果之歌》时，参考了白开元、李家真、吴笛、石真的译文。在此谨向他们表示衷心的敬意和感谢。

最后，我要向本书的责任编辑诸葛勤先生表示诚挚的感谢，我们是几十年的朋友和同事（他曾在浙江大学外语学院工作多年），他不仅是本书的责任编辑，也是我多本教材和专著的编辑或策划者。他的辛勤工作和真知灼见为我的成果增添了魅力。

黄建滨

2022 年于杭州西湖区求是村